A squall broke like a dark sheet ripping apart before their eyes

Annja suddenly saw it through the rain-streaked windscreen. A steel castle, its pylons obscured by waves and mist and blowing sheets of rain, seemed to float in the air before them.

It had been a masterful feat of flying by Tex, swinging deliberately wide of the station in order to approach from out to sea—the direction from which traffic was least likely to come. And least likely to be closely watched.

But now relief was crowded from Annja's mind by a new throng of fears. "Don't you need runway space for *Ariel* to taxi to a stop?" she asked.

"Usually," Tex replied.

"And aren't we, well, kind of low?"

"I'm bagging two birds with one cliché," he said. He had already throttled the engine suspiciously low. The ultralight wallowed in the heavy turbulent air mere feet above the waves like a moth over a flame. Suddenly, he pulled the yoke into his flat stomach. *Ariel*'s nose came up. She soared.

The grim gray cliff of steel seemed close enough to touch. Annja braced for impact.

Titles in this series:

ROGUE Angel

Alex Archer

THE LOST SCROLLS

A GOLD EAGLE BOOK FROM
WORLDWIDE®

TORONTO • NEW YORK • LONDON
AMSTERDAM • PARIS • SYDNEY • HAMBURG
STOCKHOLM • ATHENS • TOKYO • MILAN
MADRID • WARSAW • BUDAPEST • AUCKLAND

First edition May 2007

ISBN-13: 978-0-373-62124-8
ISBN-10:   0-373-62124-8

THE LOST SCROLLS

Special thanks and acknowledgment to
Victor Milan for his contribution to this work.

The
LEGEND

...THE ENGLISH COMMANDER TOOK
JOAN'S SWORD AND RAISED IT HIGH.

The broadsword, plain and unadorned,
gleamed in the firelight. He put the tip against
the ground and his foot at the center of the blade.
The broadsword shattered, fragments falling
into the mud. The crowd surged forward,
peasant and soldier, and snatched the shards
from the trampled mud. The commander tossed
the hilt deep into the crowd.
Smoke almost obscured Joan, but she continued
praying till the end, until finally the flames climbed
her body and she sagged against the restraints.

Joan of Arc died that fateful day in France,
but her legend and sword are reborn....

1

"I thought Julius Caesar burned down the Great Library," Annja Creed said. She picked her way gingerly across a small lot of churned-up dust with chunks of yellow-brick rubble in it, glad for the durability of her hiking boots. She was sheltered from the already intense morning Mediterranean sun by the floppy straw hat she wore over her yellow T-shirt and khaki cargo pants.

"He did, Ms. Creed," her handsome young Egyptian archaeologist escort said, turning to smile at her. He had a narrow, dark hawk's face and flashing eyes. His white lab smock hung from wide shoulders and flapped around the backs of his long skinny legs in the sea breeze snaking around the close-set buildings. "Among others."

"Call me Annja, please," she said.

He laughed. His teeth were as perfect as his English. His trace of accent made young Dr. Ismail al-Maghrabi seem that much more exotic. I love my job, she thought.

"If you will call me Ismail," he said.

"Done," she replied with a laugh.

Ahead of them stood a ten-foot-high loaf-shaped translucent plastic bubble. The rumbling of generators forced them to raise their voices as they approached. Some kind of structure had recently been demolished here, hard by the Alexandrian waterfront in the old Greek quarter. Big grimy warehouses and blocks of shops with cracked-stucco fronts crowded together on all sides. Although Alexandria was a major tourist destination the rumble and stink of buses and trucks through the narrow streets suggested little of charm and less of antiquity. Still, Annja's heart thumped in her throat with anticipation.

"For one thing," al-Maghrabi said, "the library was very extensive indeed. Also parts of it appear to have been scattered across the Greek quarter. As you probably know, in 2004 a team of Egyptian and Polish archaeologists uncovered a series of what appear to be lecture halls a few blocks from here."

She nodded. "I read about it on the BBC Web site at the time. A very exciting development."

"Most. The library was a most remarkable facility, as much a great university and research center as anything else. Along with the famous book collections, and of course reading rooms and auditoria, it offered dormitories for its visitors, lush gardens, even gymnasia with swimming pools."

"Really? I had no idea."

He stopped to open the latch to a door in a wooden frame set into the inflated tent. "The envelope is for climate control," he explained, opening the door for her. "Positive air pressure allows us to keep humidity and pollution at bay. Our treasures are probably not exceptionally vulnerable to such influences, considering their condition, but why take chances?"

The interior seemed gloomy after the brilliant

daylight. Annja paused to let her eyes adjust as he resecured the door. There was little to see but a hole cut into the ground. "You seem to enjoy some pretty enviable resources here, if you don't mind my saying so, Ismail."

"Not at all! Our discoveries here have attracted worldwide attention, which in turn helps to secure the resources to develop and conserve them properly. For that I believe we have to thank the Internet—and of course your own television network, which provides a share of our funding."

"Yes. I am thrilled they allowed me to come here," Annja said.

"I'm told the scrolls contain revelations about the lost civilization of Atlantis." Annja couldn't mask the skepticism in her voice.

"Come with me. I trust you don't mind a certain amount of sliding into holes in the ground?"

Annja laughed. "I am a real archaeologist, Ismail. I don't just play one on TV."

She didn't actually have to slide. A slanting tunnel about three feet wide and five feet high had been dug down to a subterranean chamber perhaps a dozen feet below ground level. Hunched over, they followed thick yellow electrical cords down the shallow ramp.

"As you no doubt know," her guide said, "the library is believed to have been built early in the third century B.C. by Ptolemy II, around the temple to the Muses built by his father, the first Ptolemy."

"That's the Mouseion, isn't it?" she said. "Origin of our word *museum?*"

"Yes. It was also said that Ptolemy III decreed that all travelers arriving in Alexandria had to surrender any books or scrolls in their possession to be copied by official scribes before being returned to them. While we don't know for certain if that is true, the library's collection swiftly grew to be the grandest in the Mediter-ranean world."

They reached a level floor of stone polished slick by many feet over many years. Banks of yellowish floodlights lit a chamber perhaps ten by twenty feet. Three people were crowded inside, two on hands and knees rooting in what appeared to be some kind of lumpy mound. One was bending over a modern table. The air was cool and smelled of soil and mildew.

The person at the table straightened and turned toward them, beaming. He was a tall, pot-bellied young man with crew-cut blond hair and an almost invisible goatee on the uppermost of his several chins. "Greetings! You must be Annja Creed."

He held out a big hand. Annja knew at once he was a working archaeologist. He looked soft and pale overall, but his hand was callused and cracked like a stonemason's, from digging, lifting and the painstaking work of chipping artifacts from a stony matrix with a dentist's steel pick.

"This is Dr. Szczepan Pilitowski," Ismail said. He struggled with the first name—it came out sounding close enough to *Stepan*. "He's our expert in extracting the scrolls safely from the ground."

"We all do what we can," Pilitowski said in a cheerful tone. "There is much to be done."

The other two, a man and a woman, turned around and picked themselves up from the floor. They wore kneepads, Annja noticed. One was a man, the other a woman. Both were thin and dark, and she took them for Egyptians.

"This is Ali Mansur and Maria Frodyma," Ismail said. The man just bobbed his head and grinned shyly.

The woman stuck out her hand. She wore her black hair in a bun, and had a bright, birdlike air to her. "Please call me Maria," she said in a Polish accent as Annja shook her hand.

"Annja."

"This was a library storeroom," Ismail said. "Most of the scrolls were kept in locked cabinets, in chambers such as this. Only the most popular items, or those specifically requested by scholars, were stored in the reading rooms."

"So that heap…?" Annja said, nodding toward the rubble mound where Maria and Ali had been working.

"The remains of a cabinet," Pilitowski said. "Damaged by the fire, it collapsed and mostly decomposed, leaving the burned scrolls behind."

"How many scrolls did the library possess?" Annja asked. "Or does anyone really know?"

"Not precisely," Maria said, wiping sweat

from her forehead with the back of one hand. She seemed to show a quick smile to the bulky and jovial Pilitowski, whose own smile broadened briefly. "Some have hypothesized it held as few as forty thousand scrolls. Others suggest the founding Ptolemy set a goal of half a million. On the basis of what we have found, we feel confident conjecturing the former limit is far too low. As to the upper—" She shrugged expressively.

"This isn't my time period," Annja confessed, believing as she did in professional full disclosure. "But I can certainly see how the recovery of any number of scrolls at all from the ancient world is a terrific thing."

"Oh, yes," Maria replied.

"And here you see three of them," Pilitowski boomed. A vast callused paw swept dramatically toward the table.

They looked like three forearm-sized chunks of wood fished out of a campfire, Annja thought. They lay on a sheet of white plastic.

"These are actual scrolls?"

"Yes, yes," Pilitowski said. "My friends and I extracted them this morning."

Annja felt a thrill. She'd seen older artifacts—she'd seen Egyptian papyri a thousand years older in the British Museum. But there was something about these scrolls, the thrill of something lost for two thousand years and believed to be indecipherable even if found. Yet modern technology was about to restore the contents of these lumps of char to the world.

"Even if they're just grocery lists," she said a little breathlessly, "this is just so exciting."

The others just smiled at her. *They* knew.

"Who really burned the library, anyway?" she asked Ismail. "Was it Julius Caesar?"

The others looked to Ismail. Ali was still grinning but had yet to utter a syllable. Annja's first thought had been that he didn't speak English. But that appeared to be the common language on the multinational dig. She began to suspect he was just shy.

"Caesar was one of the culprits," her guide said.

"One of them?"

"And not the first," Maria said. The archaeologists seemed glad of the break. Annja understood that. They loved their work, she could tell, as she loved the work when she was engaged in it. But it could be brutally arduous, and breaks were welcome.

"The first major fire damage occurred around 88 B.C.," the woman said, "when much of Alexandria burned down during civil disorders. This may have been the greatest destruction. Then during the Roman civil wars in 47 B.C., Julius Caesar chased his rival, Pompey, into the city. When Egyptian forces attacked him, Caesar set fire to the dockyards and the Egyptian fleet. The fire probably spread through trade goods piled on the docks waiting to be loaded on ships. The library lay near the waterfront, like now. Many scrolls were lost in the conflagration. Also it appears Roman soldiers stole many scrolls and sent them to Rome."

"But that wasn't the end of the library?" Annja asked.

Smiling, Ismail shook his head. "Oh, no. Only a fraction of the scrolls were lost at that time. Although we believe that this site burned then. And finally, Emperor Aurelian burned the Greek quarter in 273, when the Romans made war upon the Palmyran Queen Zenobia. That destroyed more of the library."

"So what happened to the rest of the library," Annja asked, "if fire didn't destroy it?"

"Time," Maria said.

Annja looked at the dark, diminutive archaeologist. Maria shrugged again. "Egypt's rulers lost interest in maintaining the library. Much of it simply fell into disuse. Here, as elsewhere, people reused the scrolls, or even burned them for fuel. But most simply rotted away in the heat and humidity."

"All except the ones neatly protected by a thick coating of carbonization," Ali said suddenly in a deep baritone and beautiful British accent.

Annja stared at him. He smiled but said nothing more. She suspected he'd used up his allotment of spoken words for the day.

"Ali has a second degree in biochemistry, you see," Pilitowski explained.

"Ah," Annja said.

"WELL, YOU KNOW, Annja," the young Egyptian archaeologist said as he walked with her into the huge old brick building next to the dig where the team had set up headquarters, "we make no claims concerning the veracity of the scrolls. We only recover them. And are thrilled to do it, if I may say so."

"As well you should be," she said. "It's just that Atlantis is a hot button for archaeologists in the U.S., Ismail."

Their voices echoed slightly in the enormous space. Wooden partitions had been set up to delineate work areas and offices.

"It is for all of us," he said. "We are, after all, on a quest for the truth, are we not?"

"Oh, yes," she agreed.

"And should we not follow the truth wherever it might lead us?"

"All right. I see where you're headed with this, Ismail. And you're right. If I'm going to be a serious scientist, then evidence needs to outweigh my preconceptions."

He smiled and nodded with boyishly visible relief.

"Now," she said, "let's go see this evidence."

The headquarters appeared to have spent

much of its career as a warehouse, with high walls of yellowish brick, steel struts for rafters and grimy skylights admitting brownish morning light. It smelled more than slightly of fish. Annja presumed it must be their proximity to the waterfront. The smell couldn't last decades, could it?

They walked down an aisle to an open doorway. From inside came a blast of raucous feminine laughter. Ismail's fine features tightened briefly.

He ushered Annja into a wide room, well lit by banks of standing lights. Several people worked at a row of computers. Others examined blackened-log-like scrolls on a big table.

"You might find this interesting," Ismail said, leading her toward a table. On it stood a curious device like a bundle of upright rods worked through one of the burned scrolls. "It's based on a machine invented in the eighteenth century to unroll burned papyri."

The two technicians operating it had teased out several inches of scroll. It resembled charred bark being peeled from a log. They paused to smile and nod at Annja as Ismail introduced them.

"We mostly make use of magnetic-resonance imaging to take pictures of the scrolls, layer by layer, without unrolling them," he said. "But we explore every means of recovering their content. And over here—" he turned to a wide white table where bright white underlighting illuminated the faces of the Egyptian-looking man and European-looking woman bending over it "—we have our apparatus for photographing fragments of broken scrolls we find."

What sounded like a great gong tolled. Everybody stiffened. The woman from the scroll unroller, whom Ismail introduced as Bogumila, exclaimed, "Aleksy, call Ali and Szczepan and Maria. Tell them to come quickly!"

One of the pair at the photo table took out a cell phone and whipped it open. He spoke quickly in Polish.

Others were beginning to arrive on the run from the other cubicles. Apparently the gong, which she guessed was a recording, was turned up high to let everyone in the converted warehouse know there was news.

Everyone crowded before a large flat-screen monitor. An image had appeared, a ragged off-white oblong, with spidery dark gray markings on it that Annja guessed might be ancient Greek. "*Da!*" somebody exclaimed.

A young woman sat perched on a stool by the photographic table, at the other end from the bulky camera itself, which was mounted on a heavy mobile stand. Now she pushed off and came sauntering over. She was strikingly pretty, with pale blond hair done in pigtails that made her round-cheeked face look even younger than it probably was. Her eyes were big and blue, if currently half-lidded as if with contemptuous disinterest. She wore a tight black-and-red top that showed off her healthy figure and an extremely short skirt with horizontal stripes in red and black. For all the horizontal stripes and harsh colors she was stunning looking; Annja fought down an inclination to hate her.

As she approached the flat-screen monitor Annja felt uneasy. China-doll perfect the young woman's appearance may have been, but she gave a strong impression of negativity.

Excited as they were, the other team members moved back from the screen as she approached. The young woman leaned in, jaw working on a wad of gum.

"Not too close, Jadzia," the man at the keyboard said. "You are the anticomputer geek."

She gave him a baleful squint and snapped her gum at him. She stuck a finger toward the screen. The guy at the keyboard seemed to wind up tighter and tighter the closer her fingertip, the nail painted black, got. She read in a bored voice:

"—had in their possession most marvelous stones, like unto gemstones, such as rubies or emeralds, but the size of goose's eggs, wherein they stored a force as potent as the lightnings. Perhaps this blasphemy, this stealing of the very thunder of mighty Zeus, evoked his wrath and caused him to cast down that which belonged by right to Poseidon."

She shrugged, popped her gum, straightened up with a little headflip. "That's it for this page. The break was a physical one. Nothing to translate."

Everybody cheered and hugged each other and exchanged high fives. Annja noticed nobody tried to embrace the pigtailed blond girl.

"Can she really just read it like that?" Annja asked the air.

She didn't expect to be answered in the hubbub. But beside her boomed the ever-cheerful voice of Dr. Pilitowski. "Ah, yes, she can. This is the noted Jadzia Arkadczyk. She holds degrees in cryptology and linguistics. She has a remarkable gift for languages. She is, quite simply, beyond genius."

Annja studied the young woman, who seemed content to stand looking offhandedly at the screen, soaking up the arm's-length adulation of her comrades. Annja had her own gift for languages. It had formed a key part of her love for travel and adventure.

"I'm impressed," she said.

Maria was speaking to the girl and nodding at

Annja. Jadzia turned and looked at the visitor for the first time. Her blue eyes flew wide.

"I know you!" she exclaimed. "I have seen you on *Chasing History's Monsters*."

"Well, yes, I appear on the show from time to time," Annja said with authentic modesty. She did not want to be known primarily for her association with the program. Especially among peers as distinguished as these.

"You are the woman they bring on when they wish to cover something up," the girl went on, voice rising accusatorily, "and undo all the good work done by poor Kristie Chatham!"

2

"They despised everything but virtue," Annja read, the bubbly water, still hot, gurgling to the slight motions of her body as she kept the book braced open against her drawn-up knees.

Photographic specialist Rahim al-Haj had lent her a copy of Plato's *Dialogues,* well grimed and dog-eared by the team, as she took her leave of the recovery site late that afternoon. Unwinding in her hotel room after dinner in one of her favorite fashions, she was reading what Plato had written about Atlantis.

The legend claimed there had been an island outside the Pillars of Heracles, "larger than

Libya and Asia put together." Whatever Plato meant by Asia. A big island, to be sure.

The Atlanteans, the story said, made war on Europe. The Athenians, eventually standing alone, had defeated them. Then violent earthquakes had occurred, followed by floods. In a single day and night the island of Atlantis and all its people disappeared in the depths of the sea. That sounded pretty final to Annja. It did intrigue her that the Athenians apparently suffered greatly from the same catastrophe.

"You never hear that part of the myth when people talk about Atlantis," she said aloud.

There was a lot of discussion about the founding of Athens. It intrigued Annja to read of what seemed to her to be an equality of men and women in ancient Athens, including in warfare. She was also struck by the claim that Greece had once been a wonderfully green and fertile peninsula that had suffered sorely from millennia of soil erosion. She wondered if there might be something to that part, anyway.

At last the narrative wandered around to Atlantis. It had been built by the sea god Poseidon to impress his human love, Cleito. It was a land of fertile fields, concentric circles of canals, elephants, that sort of thing. She made note of several details to take up with her hosts in the morning.

What made the biggest impression on her was the interval of nine thousand years since the supposed fall of Atlantis. She put her book up on the rim of the sink and closed her eyes and tried to wrap her mind around it.

As someone who had studied geology, and a bit of paleontology, as part of her formal education, she had little trouble coping with nine millennia. In geologic terms it was a fraction of a second.

But for a coherent account of events to survive for nine thousand years—for any kind of knowledge to be transmitted over such a yawning gulf of time—that just made her jaw sag in disbelief.

She was well aware that archeology, especially the relatively new but fruitful practice of applying modern forensic techniques to archeological evidence, was showing that as often as not the written histories bore only a passing resemblance to what could be physically demonstrated to have really happened. History was perhaps not bunk—not altogether. But to say it was inexact was like saying it snows at the North Pole.

Could any meaningful, let alone accurate, information be transmitted over nine thousand years? She doubted it.

And yet…the legend of Atlantis had persisted all that time. It had exercised a fascination on the human imagination continuously since Plato had recorded it. Does that count for something?

She shook her head. Weariness was getting the better of her. She'd been going pretty hard of late, to say the least. She stood up with a slog of water and a cascade of soapy foam down her long smooth body and legs, and drew the curtain around the tub to shower off before heading to bed.

IT WAS LATE AT NIGHT. Annja had spent the day down in the excavation itself, painstakingly helping to extract burned scrolls from the rubble of the burned cabinets. She was exhausted and felt sticky from sweat, although here in the main lab inside the old warehouse it was quite cool. Apparently the Supreme Council on Antiquities was willing to spring for air-conditioning. Or maybe the television network was springing for it—she was grateful to whomever.

She noticed Jadzia lurking off to one side. The girl was fanning herself with a sheaf of fan-folded paper and trying to chat up a handsome young Egyptian technician working on a computer near her. Either he was shy or deliberately ignoring her. She caught Annja's attention, glared and looked away.

"Correct me if I'm wrong," Annja said, propping her rump on a table. "Wasn't the Minoan civilization destroyed by a great big volcanic eruption around 1500 B.C.?"

"Yes," Pilitowski said. "The catastrophic eruption of Thera. It is now estimated to have been at least ten times as powerful as Krakatau in 1883."

"Although geologists tend to date the eruption from about 1600 B.C.," Aleksy Fabiszak, the team's geology specialist, said. "That volume of ejecta would be the same magnitude as the terrible Tambora eruption of 1815, the most violent of recorded history."

"One point on the volcanic explosivity scale beneath supervolcano," Maria said.

"So it would have made a royal mess of much of the Aegean," Annja said. "I mean, the way the catastrophe that destroyed Atlantis is supposed to have?"

"Well, if what you're getting at is that perhaps Atlantis and the Minoan culture of Crete were the same," Pilitowski said, "a lot of people have come to suspect that."

Jadzia snapped her gum loudly. "*Somebody* should tell her," she said brassily, as if Annja were not in the room, "that we have found many references on the scrolls that make it impossible the writer was talking about the Minoans."

Burly, good-natured Dr. Pilitowski looked to the slight, dark Maria, who shrugged. Annja got the impression she wasn't the only one who found the brilliant language expert a problem child.

"From contextual evidence in what we have translated of these Atlantis scrolls," Maria said, "it is clear they were written about half a century after Solon. That would make them a century older than Plato's writing."

"So far we are not finding any reference to Solon at all," Naser said. He was a plump, pallid man in his thirties with a neat beard, who spoke with a Lower East Side New York accent. "We suspect that somewhere along the line different end-of-the-world stories got mixed together."

"Hmm," Annja said. She was still having trouble dealing with serious archaeologists taking Atlantis seriously. Although she had to admit none of them actually seemed to be vested in the *truth* of the scrolls, even if they did call them the Atlantis scrolls. But there was no mistaking the excitement that ran through the site whenever the gong went off to announce that they had images of more restored fragments.

"One thing I'm puzzled by," she said, "is that reading Plato, I didn't really see any talk about advanced technology. Not like what people always talk about, with flying machines and artificial light and all that."

"That actually seems to have first appeared in

a book called *A Dweller on Two Planets,* which came out late in the nineteenth century," Pilitowski said. "Its author claimed to have received the information in dreams."

Annja raised an eyebrow.

"Well, channeled it, actually." He shrugged. "What can I say? He was from California."

"Somebody ought to tell her the new scrolls substantiate much of what Frederick Oliver wrote in that book," Jadzia said hotly.

Annja looked to Pilitowski, who shrugged. "I do not know that I would go so far as to say 'substantiate,'" he said. "Nonetheless, we must admit we find certain correspondences."

"We began to wonder if some alternate account of Atlantis might have surfaced sporadically throughout history," Naser said, "without impinging on academic scholarship. And that Oliver got hold of it somehow."

"With all respect," Annja said, "that seems to be reaching a bit far."

"Not so far as believing in channeling," Naser said.

"True," Annja said with a laugh.

Annja looked sidelong at Jadzia. The young woman—she just acts like a girl, Annja thought—posed a conundrum. For one thing, Annja wasn't used to evoking knee-jerk hostility in people she hadn't met. It bothered her. She led an isolated enough existence that she felt threatened when somebody reacted to her with such vehement negativity, as if perhaps she had at last been found out as invalid and unworthy for human companionship.

For all her rigorous training in cryptology, which Annja knew was no soft science, involving some of the most abstruse and demanding maths around, Jadzia clung to the role of true believer in Atlantis mysteries and doubtless a thousand other conspiracy theories. She wasn't the first person Annja had bumped up against who harbored both serious scientific credentials and crackpot beliefs. She sometimes suspected that really high-level scientists could only be expected to be sane and knowledgeable in their own field of expertise, and anything else was fair game.

So maybe Jadzia's hostility arose from antipathy toward the role Annja played, authentically enough, of house skeptic and counterpoint to Kristie Chatham, who believed in everything.

Annja had certainly suffered many flame attacks from such antifans before she quit visiting the show's message boards, despite the insistent entreaties of her producer, Doug Morrell, that she do so. But that virulence didn't spill out of cyberspace into her lap.

She suddenly remembered something odd said in passing the day before. "Why do they call Jadzia the anticomputer geek?" she asked Maria. Very softly, she thought.

But apparently among Jadzia's attributes was a very keen sense of hearing. "I kill computers," she announced proudly, her voice sharp edged.

"How?" Annja asked. "With a sledgehammer?"

She hadn't meant to say that—really. But instead of flaring up at the comment, or the laughter it evoked from the eight or so other team members in the large room, Jadzia laughed louder and more brazenly than the others.

"Just by touching," she said proudly.

Annja cocked an eyebrow at Pilitowski, who

shrugged a big sloped shoulder. "It is true," he said. "We cannot let her handle anything electronic. In seconds—" he snapped his fingers "—pfft!"

"It has to do with my personal magnetic field," Jadzia said. She wore schoolgirl blue and white, with knee-high white stockings instead of the thigh-highs she'd had on the day before. Her skirt wasn't any longer. "It disrupts electronic devices."

"I don't buy that," Annja said. "Things like that don't happen in the real world."

"Lend me your cell phone?" the blond woman purred.

The gong sounded so loudly Annja jumped.

ONLY TWO OF THE team members were on duty down in the current excavation—a short, stocky Polish man named Tadeusz and a willowy Egyptian woman a head taller named Haditha, who wore what looked like a ruby in her pierced left nostril. The pair had trouble communicating verbally, since neither's English was the strongest. Haditha spoke beautiful French. Tadeusz was a bit hard of hearing into the bargain. Yet they worked well together, seeming to have evolved some brand of nonverbal communication.

Everyone tacitly assumed they were sleeping together, although they never seemed to seek each other out off-hours. The consensus held that this was a cunning pose. Annja, knowing what a hotbed of intrigue and gossip the best-ordered dig could turn into after only a couple of weeks, reserved judgment. Like everyone else archaeologists loved a good story, and were reluctant to let facts spoil it—outside their chosen area of expertise, of course.

They came out of the bubble tent on the run. A few bright lights shone randomly from the nearby buildings, casting jagged patterns of light and shadow across the demolition rubble. As they went in the door of the former warehouse, Haditha heard a peculiar double cough from behind. The noises had an edge, reminiscent of knuckles on hardwood.

Tadeusz pitched forward on his face on the floor beside her. She stared at him in astonishment. The back of his pale head was stained dark and wet.

3

A sound behind Haditha made her turn. She gasped at a black insectile figure looming over her.

The man in the night-vision goggles and blackout gear stuck the thick muzzle of his sound-suppressed machine pistol against her sternum and fired the same precise 2-round burst his partner had used on the Polish archaeologist an instant before. Haditha recoiled, then simply collapsed, her dark almond eyes rolling up in her head.

From high above and in front of the black-clad pair came small muffled crashes, themselves hardly louder than coughs. Shards of glass descended from above, swooping like falling leaves, breaking to smaller pieces on the black rubber runner that ran along the central aisle. More black-clad figures rappelled from the broken skylights.

WITH A FROWN Annja snapped her head up from where she leaned close to the big flat-screen monitor. "What was that noise?"

Most of the team members ignored her. A number of new images were coming in from scrolls shipped intact to the jet propulsion laboratory, where layered MRI scans were used to extract the writing from within the rolled papyri.

A couple of the Egyptian team members murmured briefly in Arabic.

"Probably just some homeless," Naser said.

However, Ismail, who had just come in, turned and started back out the door into the darkened aisle.

"Wait!" Annja heard him cry in English. "You cannot come in here!"

She heard two sounds like blows of a distant tack hammer.

THROUGH THE USE of handheld terahertz radar units, which enabled them to see right through walls, the raiders knew precisely where every member of the Polish-Egyptian dig team was located.

As more of their fellows dropped in, the pair who had taken down the first two targets spread out to secure the entryway. The rest slipped in quick, silent pairs into the side cubicles. More double thumps sounded as they cleared them.

The Nomex-clad raiders in their goggles and face masks knew there was no escape from the large room at the end of the aisle. The big windows throughout the structure had all been bricked shut long ago.

It would be the perfect killing floor.

"GET DOWN!" Annja shouted.

Recent experience had brought her to the conclusion that people dressed in black Nomex and masks and carrying automatic weapons were not in a state of mind to be reasoned with.

Jadzia was already in motion, grabbing the blackened-log papyri from the table and stuffing them in a large lime-green-and-purple gym bag that was used to ferry bagged artifacts.

Ismail staggered a step back into the lab. Then he rallied and lurched forward to stand with arms braced in the door. He called something defiant sounding in Arabic that ended in an agonized cough.

Annja circled rapidly to her right. She knew they were trapped. Her only hope of saving any of the team from the attack she already knew was in progress was to get out of the immediate line of fire and hope to ambush intruders as they entered.

They were too far ahead of her.

Ismail reeled into a table and spun, the front of his shirt and white coat seemingly tie-dyed in florets of red. He pitched onto his face as a pair of men in black stepped through the door and then to opposite sides. They held 2-round machine pistols to their shoulders.

The one to Annja's left fired a two-shot burst into Szczepan Pilitowski from six feet away. The big archaeologist fell heavily. The other aimed at Annja. She had already reversed and was racing toward the far end of the room. Bullets knocked masonry dust from the raw wall behind her. The ricochets moaned like restless ghosts.

Another black-clad killer appeared firing in the doorway as Annja, taking and holding a deep breath, hit Jadzia in a flying tackle and knocked her beyond the end of the long table on which the computers sat. The girl yelped in surprise but had the presence of mind to keep clutching the satchel of scrolls with both hands.

Annja heard bullets punching into computer cases with an almost musical rhythm. The team members screamed or called out hoarsely as they died. There was no chance. The killers were professional enough to ensure that. They had no means of fighting back and nowhere to flee.

Leaving Jadzia sprawled in the relative shelter between the end of the computer table and a round-topped, bricked-up window in the end wall, Annja sprang up onto the table. The killers were moving into the room, fanning out to hunt down team members trying to hide behind filing cabinets and under tables.

An intruder raised his weapon to Annja. She threw the nearest computer case at him. Power and video cables ripped noisily out from the rear. It struck him in the goggles and knocked him backward against the wall.

Bullets struck the wall near her. She hoisted the accompanying computer monitor end over end at the shooter.

The monitor was not a flat-screen. It was an old-fashioned model and weighed a good forty-five pounds. The man gave up on shooting to raise his hands defensively. Annja heard his ulna snap. The shooter went over backward with a crash.

The other three men opened up on her. Annja dived off the table toward the side wall. Her foot came down on some kind of power converter or adaptor and flew right out from under her. Her head cracked into the wall. Her teeth clacked painfully. Red sparks flew behind her eyes.

"I got her," she heard a man say, his voice muffled by his mask. Head spinning, she found herself on all fours, too dizzy to rise. She raised her head at the man in black aiming the machine pistol at her. The hole in the end looked big enough to swallow her whole.

A figure loomed up behind the black-clad killer. Before the gunman could fire, Szczepan

Pilitowski, his wide pale face streaming blood, struck him from behind with a chair.

The two intruders still on their feet opened fire from the far side of the room. Though the suppressed shots sounded relatively loud in the enclosed space, they were not loud enough to mask the hard thumps of the bullets hitting the big archaeologist's soft body. He roared in defiance, turning toward them. Then his legs gave way. He fell to the floor with a slapping sound.

The man Pilitowski clubbed lay sprawled on his face with a pool of dark red spreading out from his head.

Annja yanked loose his MP-5. Shouldering it, she came up to a crouch. The weapon had open battle sights.

The killers had lost track of her when she jumped off the table. They were making plenty of noise and she could actually differentiate where both men were. When she popped up from behind the table, the MP-5's ghost-ring sights were lined up almost perfectly on the shooter to her left.

She aimed for the man's head and fired. The night-vision goggles shattered. The killer let his weapon drop on its long sling, covered his face with his hands and fell onto the photography table. It upset, spilling priceless blackened chunks of ancient lore to the floor.

Annja ducked as the other man blazed away at her. More computer cases crashed as bullets punched through them, scrambling the delicate circuit boards inside.

She rose up on all fours, still clutching the machine pistol, scrabbled forward like a monkey across the prone body of the man Pilitowski had hit. She turned around the long computer table and launched herself in a forward slide on her left side across the center aisle.

She held the pistol grip tight. She figured the gunman's torso was encased in some kind of body armor so she chopped his legs out from under him. He fell screaming and kicking, spraying blood.

The machine pistol's charging handle locked back. Empty. Annja slid into the collapsed photo table and stopped.

From the darkened corridor outside she heard shouts. Bullets glanced off the concrete floor near her outspread legs and ricocheted around the room. Their tumbling made them scream.

She heard a shrill yowl of fury from the back of the lab.

She jumped up, risked gunfire in a dash back across the aisle, and vaulted the computer table. The man she had thrown the computer into had found his feet if not his firearm. He was staggering toward Jadzia, who had her back against the wall and the satchel clutched protectively to her breasts. The intruder held a big black saw-backed knife in his hand.

He heard Annja land behind him, and spun. His hand lashed out horizontally with the combat knife.

He was way short. Annja didn't even have to dodge. Before he could recover with a back stroke she sprang like an angry leopard and closed with him. She grabbed him by the biceps of his knife arm and his left shoulder.

Something came skittering down the aisle into the middle of the lab.

Grenade. Annja was out of time, with nowhere to go.

In fear and frustrated anger, Annja stepped past the black-clad assassin like a dancer leading her partner, and threw him toward the back of the room with all her strength. He hit the sealed-off window with a crunch. The bricks exploded outward into the humid Alexandrian night.

Grabbing the motionless Jadzia around her narrow waist, Annja dragged the young woman to the window and leaped out through the hole in the wall.

The grenade exploded behind her, filling the lab with smoke and tear gas.

Annja landed hard in the alley behind the building. Her right ankle buckled, not quite far enough to sprain. Her knee slammed against something hard—a bottle or stone.

"What are you doing?" Jadzia screamed from under arm. "Put me down!"

Annja dropped her, eliciting a fresh squall of fury. They were in a space ten feet wide between the warehouse and the next building. Lights shone from a crane out by the docks a long block away. A fast glance over her shoulder showed only dark the other way.

The hunters had night-vision equipment. Light gave her at least equal vision and the possibility, however slight, of witnesses.

A slim edge was an edge.

"Come on," she said to Jadzia, who was sitting up rubbing grit out of her hair and cursing in several languages Annja didn't recognize.

Jadzia opened her mouth to say something, probably a snotty protest. Annja grabbed her arm and started running. With a squawk the young woman found herself dragged to her feet and scrambling, still clutching the satchel.

As Annja reached the alley's end a figure loomed before her. The bizarre shape of the head silhouetted against the silvery glare told her all she needed to know.

Letting go of Jadzia's wrist, she sprinted the last few yards at full speed and leaped in the air as the inevitable machine pistol came up. Her right leg pistoned out in a flying side kick. It telescoped the single objective tube of the night-vision goggles and snapped the gunman's neck as if he'd been hit in the face with a pile driver. In a sense he had.

Annja landed beyond the body, out on the rubble field. The inflatable tent over the excavation was ahead and to her right. She did a quick scan of the area. She seemed to be alone. The intruders, knowing there were no exits from the converted warehouse but the front way in, apparently and logically hadn't bothered leaving more than one man on guard outside. Annja stood drawing in huge breaths of thick Mediterranean air flavored with cooking spices and motor oil.

A crunch of shoes on the loose, gritty earth behind brought her around. Jadzia was teetering toward her with blue eyes wide.

"What the hell?" she said.

"I'm scared, pissed off and alive," Annja said. "And damned determined to stay that way. If you want to do the same, come with me. And don't ask questions till later!"

4

Jadzia swiveled her pigtailed head from side to side as the two women walked down a street full of hulking trucks. The narrow lane ran between big dark warehouse walls near the Western Harbor wharves. It smelled strongly of seawater and sealife uncomfortably past its sell-by date. Water sloshed along the rough surface underfoot. Not even her college geology courses enabled Annja Creed to know whether the street was actual cobblestone or just really decrepit pavement.

They passed through a spill of light from the rectangular opening into an amber-lit cavern of a warehouse. Rough-looking men in badly stained coveralls stood around the entrance smoking and talking in guttural Arabic while a skinny young man, probably just a boy, dressed in a black T-shirt and baggy cotton shorts reeled in a big hose. The smell of fish was very strong.

The conversation stream trickled to a stop as the men saw the pair of Western women, one dressed skimpily enough to be considered more than a little risqué even in cosmopolitan Alexandria.

Annja smiled widely and nodded at the startled male faces as they passed through the island of light. Nothing to see here, she thought, trying hard to broadcast it despite her devoted disbelief in psychic powers. Mess with us and you'll be trying to digest your teeth. Have a nice night!

She had to tug extra hard at Jadzia's wrist to tow her the rest of the way out of the light.

Jadzia followed her none-too-gentle insistence. The young language prodigy continued to maintain the shocked silence that had settled over her after Annja had killed the final attacker standing between them and escape. Fortunately, Jadzia showed little difficulty with the hike. Either she wasn't one of those nerds who was totally opposed to any physical activity greater than teetering to the bathroom or the fridge to get another can of Red Bull, or adrenaline was working its magic. As aggravatingly lean as she was, Annja suspected the former.

Annja led them west for about a mile, following the waterfront, through the Greek quarter and into the city's west side. She stayed alert but saw no sign they were being tailed. At length she circled back toward her own hotel.

"Why are we here?" Jadzia asked, looking up at the front of the hotel.

It was a modest three-star kind of place in the Greek quarter, big enough to have an elevator, a bar and even pretty decent bathrooms in all the rooms, but without being part of a big chain.

"I thought I'd grab my gear," Annja said.

Jadzia hung back. Somewhere among the nighttime streets Annja had quit having to pull her along by the wrist. She had followed on her own, and now reminded Annja uncomfortably of a lost puppy.

"But won't they know to look for us here?"

"Watch a lot of spy movies, do you?" Annja said. She instantly regretted the snide tone.

But Jadzia, while she had a flash-fire temper for *perceived* slights, proved to be dense as one of the city's ancient stone Sphinxes when a *real* one hit her. She smiled happily.

"Of course!" Her pigtails bobbed as she nodded enthusiastically. "I know all about these things."

What have I gotten myself into now? Annja wondered. "I'm betting they either aren't aware of my existence or haven't identified me yet," she said. "Your team roster is available on the Web for all to see. My name's not on it."

She knew it was thin, as she watched a cab pull under the portico. The uniformed doorman bowed as a silk-suited Sikh with silver in his beard, and his shorter companion, voluptuous in an emerald-green dress, exited the vehicle and entered the hotel. She wondered briefly what the story was. The couple dressed nicely enough to afford a much pricier place.

Annja wanted to get in and out before much could go wrong even if the night's assassins were watching for her. They might have spotted her while surveilling the dig—probably had, she had to admit to herself as she formed her plan. She would gather her things, then duck out of the hotel, shake anybody trying to tail them and head for a new place to hole up for the night.

She wasn't that attached to the belongings she had brought. She traveled light, and nowadays always packed with the expectation she might have to leave anything behind and walk away for survival's sake. Even her laptop was relatively cheap and contained no information that could easily be used against her.

But it would be convenient to have her stuff. And she reckoned that if she threw some of her own clothes on Jadzia, no matter how bad they fit her coltish form, they would be a lot less conspicuous than having the girl wandering around dressed in such a *look-at-me* manner.

"Tell you what," Annja said to Jadzia, who was rocking back and forth on her heels and chewing on her lower lip. "You keep an eye out for anybody suspicious. Okay?"

Jadzia's eyes lit up. "Okay!"

"TWO MEN in the lobby," Jadzia said. "They sit on the far side with their backs to the door and pretend to read newspapers."

"You're kidding," Annja said. She fought her irritation with the girl in the close confines of the stairway.

Jadzia's pigtails swung from side to side beneath the backward Tulane Green Wave ball cap she had stuffed down over them as she shook her head emphatically. She wore an outsized windbreaker that covered her hands, and running pants cinched as tight around her waist as they could be. They resembled a pair of gray terry-cloth sandbags.

At least playing spy got Jadzia too excited either for panic or to take potshots at Annja. Annja opened her mouth to question her further, unsure as to whether to trust the young woman's judgment. Clearly she had a taste for melo-drama. Would she see danger where it wasn't?

Annja shut her mouth. Belatedly it hit her that a degreed cryptologist might actually have a certain bent for spying.

"Right," she said. "We'll go out the back."

So I was wrong, she thought, frowning at the back of her own windbreaker as Jadzia pushed through swinging utility doors. I guess they did make me. I still have a lot to learn about this whole intrigue thing.

Little wiry Egyptian men and women looked at the brisk Western women as they passed through the hotel's service areas. Jadzia swung along like the health department inspector. Annja followed down the corridor, which smelled of steam and fresh laundry and cooking food, smiling in what she hoped was a friendly rather than nervous manner.

No one challenged them until a door flew open just in front of Annja. A man in a sort of iridescent brown suit tumbled out right in front of her wearing sunglasses and—

"A fez?" Annja said aloud.

The man's hand dived into his suit coat, which looked as if it had been intentionally made to look slightly greasy. That was all Annja needed. She acted instinctively and grabbed the upper biceps of what she figured had to be his gun arm to control it. She used the leverage to drive a forward elbow-smash into his face with her right arm. She felt impact that jarred clear down to her tailbone, and felt a sharp pain in her own arm.

The man gave up doing whatever he was doing to clutch his face. He fell straight on the floor, bleeding, to the accompaniment of thrashing and mewling noises, she thought.

"Damn," Annja said, inspecting her right elbow. A tooth had gouged her, drawing blood. She was mighty glad of her strong immune system. Human bites are nasty, she thought.

Jadzia faced Annja across the man's kicking form, eyes big. "It's Egypt," she said. "They wear fezzes. Get over it. Watch out!"

Somebody grabbed Annja from behind in a bear hug that pinned her upper arms to her rib cage. He felt big and smelled of sweat and garlic.

"I got her," he said in thickly accented English.

He hoisted her feet clear off the cracked linoleum. She felt hot breath on the back of her head, snapped it back hard. She felt, as well as heard, the cartilage of his nose shift. He grunted and his grip on her rib cage slackened.

She thrust her arms forcefully out before her,

busting the rest of the way loose. As the corrugated soles of her trusty hiking boots touched down she braced, covered her right fist with her left palm and, spinning clockwise, pile-drove an elbow into a big soft belly.

The elbow was working for her. Her attacker doubled over with a great expulsion of hot, foul-smelling air. Annja took a step to her left and side-kicked the big Egyptian. The force propelled him into a dumbwaiter that stood open in the cracked pink stucco wall to his right. The door dropped on him.

She turned around quickly to see if anybody else wanted to play. She and Jadzia had the corridor to themselves. The hotel maintenance staff did not get paid to intervene heroically in these little disputes among the guests.

She turned back.

The first man she had dropped lay on the floor moaning. His face was covered with blood. He had his hand in his jacket again.

Annja did not think he was scratching an itch. Irritably she kicked him on the point of his chin. His head, which still had the fez crammed on top of it, snapped into the wall beside him. The fez fell off. He slumped.

Annja crouched quickly, reached a bit tentatively into the clamminess of the inside of his biliously colored jacket and fished out a Beretta. Straightening, she dried the grips off with two quick swipes across the rump of her jeans. Then she pulled the slide back far enough for a flash of yellow brass to confirm he had a round chambered.

"Insurance," she said to Jadzia, whose eyes had gotten even bigger. It was true. She knew that it would be a lot easier to explain shooting an assailant to the local authorities than carving him up with a sword.

"What's wrong with a fez?" Jadzia asked.

Annja blinked and shook her head once, violently, as if trying to shed water. "It was just way too *Casablanca*," she said. "Let's just get out of here, okay?"

5

"I think it was the Muslim Brotherhood," Annja said.

"Nonsense," Jadzia replied. Beyond her, cars swished up and down the boulevard. Across the street tourists sauntered down a broad walkway that ran along the Alexandrian waterfront. "I heard one of the men shout at you in French."

"That doesn't mean anything," Annja said. "Plenty of Muslims speak French."

It was late morning. They had survived the night, at least, in a small, somewhat seedy hotel. Fortunately Annja had spent enough time knocking around the world from undergrad days onward to appreciate the fact that it was still pretty plush by Third World standards.

Jadzia had recovered from her shock—or perhaps the thrill of playing adventure spy girl—enough to gripe about the surroundings, from the mildewy smells to the stains on the bedspread.

But once she had slurped down her first mug of strong coffee well charged with sugar, and chomped her way through her first flaky pastry at the sidewalk café on the Corniche, Jadzia found something that appealed to her even more than pouting. Arguing.

Her pretty lips were twisted in a sneer as if she'd forgotten Annja had repeatedly saved her life the night before.

"They were assassins sent by the big oil companies," Jadzia said in a tone that clearly declared Annja was a moron not to recognize the facts. "They sent them to keep the knowledge of Atlantean energy secrets covered up from the world."

Annja didn't react for a moment. She was struck by the fact that the lips sneering at her were covered in a carefully applied layer of lipstick. And as far as Annja knew, Jadzia had no personal effects except her wallet, some credit cards, identification and her passport.

Do I have lipstick that shade? she wondered. The truth was she seldom bothered with it, or makeup in general, except for special events. She realized belatedly she had with her a sort of premade kit—the Mr. Right Emergency Kit— provided to her by her female cronies from *Chasing History's Monsters*. She had never, so far as she could recall, used it. Or so much as opened it.

I hope there weren't condoms in it, she thought.

"Wait," she said. Jadzia's last statement had finally penetrated her protective shields of puzzlement. "You're blaming the oil companies?"

Jadzia nodded.

"Isn't that a conspiracy theory?"

"Aren't we victims of a conspiracy?" Jadzia said in infuriatingly superior tones. "Or do you really think that those men all just independently decided to attack us last night, and wound up doing so all at the same time by coincidence? That's just stupid."

Annja frowned. It made the snottiness immeasurably worse, somehow, when the brat being snotty was *right*. At least about that angle of conspiracy. Obviously someone had conspired to hit the Polish-Egyptian dig team last night. And they'd done a hell of a job. Had it not been for the fact that she was getting used to coming under attack, they would have made a clean sweep.

Annja's fork halted halfway to her mouth. She lowered the chunk of fluffy French pastry with frosting just melting off in the Alexandrian morning heat back to her plate. She felt her stomach do a slow roll. *So many,* she thought desolately.

She saw the faces of the dead. The beatnik-looking Naser, darkly pretty Maria, cheerful Szczepan Pilitowski, who had died giving Annja a chance to save Jadzia, the scrolls and herself. Ismail—Dr. Maghrabi—who had tried to shield them all with his body, and had been ruthlessly gunned down.

Is this what it means to carry the sword? a lonely child's voice asked from the wilderness of Annja's mind. She already knew the answer.

She could hear the gruff voice of her some-time mentor, Roux's, trying to encompass cynicism and compassion at once, saying, "You cannot save the whole world, child." And she knew that was true, too.

But can't I even save those within reach of my arm?

"See?" Jadzia crowed, sipping at her coffee. "You have no answers for me."

Anger spiked in Annja. She held her body as still as if it were encased in concrete, did not allow the anger to travel so far as her eyes. Jadzia's malice was the petty malice of a spoiled child, she reminded herself. Innocent malice, if there was such a thing.

And surely there was. By no stretch of her vivid imagination could Annja see Jadzia setting about the callous murder of a dozen helpless, harmless men and women. Her petty rudeness belonged in a different universe from such an act.

Oddly, the very act of restraining herself from lashing back at Jadzia made Annja feel better. "I still think it was most likely Muslim fanatics," she said in an only slightly constricted voice.

"Why would they attack our dig? Why would they care?" Jadzia asked. "We've never heard a peep from Islamists. No threats, not anything. And the Muslim Brotherhood has very much to do already."

Such as waging an increasingly successful campaign to dislodge the fairly secular Egyptian government, Annja thought. She already saw the sand leaking out of her theory anyway. She had knocked around, and been knocked around of late, enough to have uncomfortably firsthand knowledge of Western special-operations gear. The attackers had worn Western-style blackout dress and night-vision goggles, and carried the generic Western counterterrorism weapon, the MP-5. Presumably the Muslim Brotherhood could buy that stuff and learn to use it. Even at Western expense, given the enormous amounts of military aid and training the U.S. gave Egypt. But for a group as determinedly old-fashioned as the Brotherhood, it seemed distinctly out of character.

Annja took a last sip of her mostly cooled coffee and stood up. "I need to move," she said. "Getting the blood flowing will help me think."

"THEY CONSPIRED against us," Jadzia said again. She dangled her long legs over a parapet of rough dressed stone. Several stories below lay a little shelf of rubble at the base of the citadel wall, and then the water of the Eastern Harbor, slogging and frothing.

Annja paced the terrace behind the Polish girl. White gravel crunched beneath her soles, and she could practically feel the afternoon sun beating on the wide brim of her hat with angry fists. She tried not to think of the risks Jadzia was subjecting herself to. While signs in various languages placed at intervals warned against precisely what the girl was doing, enforcement of safety rules did not seem to constitute a priority for whatever agency had charge of the big, blocky, fifteenth-century fortress of Qait-Bey. Nobody had yelled at her to get down. As for Annja, she already understood that the only way to get Jadzia to stop doing what she was doing was to try to physically prevent her. And the last thing they needed was to draw attention to themselves by getting into a fight.

Actually, the *very* last thing they needed was

for them both to get arrested for causing a public disturbance at a national monument. Her estimate of the Alexandrian police was such that she expected it might take them only seconds to sell the young women to whoever it was who wanted them so dead.

"Why do you blame the oil companies?" Annja asked. She hated to feed Jadzia's probable paranoia. But she was out of other answers, and a brisk walk through winding streets and out to the tip of the peninsula through growing morning heat hadn't done a damned thing to replenish her stock. Although Jadzia's constant whining was at least a bit of a distraction, she had to admit.

"They have the most to lose from what we might discover," the young Polish woman said.

Annja stopped and looked at her. "What did you *find* in those scrolls, anyway?"

Jadzia shrugged and kicked the heels of her tennis shoes against the yellow sandstone. They were the only part of her ensemble of the night before Annja had let her keep. "You were there for one of the most tantalizing parts."

"That bit about the crystals? That just sounded like New Age craziness warmed over."

Jadzia laughed. "Right. Twenty-five hundred years old is very new."

"But, I mean, that charging-crystals stuff—"

"We found more earlier. It spoke of all those things you found so funny—flying chariots, artificial lights, lances of light. The ancient Greek who wrote those scrolls, who somewhere got a much purer version of the story than Solon passed down to Critias, he did not have the language of technology to describe an artificial power source. He probably didn't understand it. Some kind of divine gift, like Zeus's lightnings chained, would be the closest he could come to expressing it."

"But using gemstones for batteries," Annja said. "I'm no physicist, but that sounds pretty implausible."

An Air France Airbus climbed past them from its takeoff roll, momentarily blanking out the conversation in the scream of its engines. "What?" Annja shouted.

"I said, how would that airplane strike an

ancient Greek? Implausible, yes? Everything is impossible until someone does it."

Annja sought an answer to that and could find none that didn't ring as hollow as a pewter doubloon. *Come on*, she told herself. Is she really that much smarter than I am? Or am I letting myself get intimidated, just because everyone told me what a supergenius she was?

Annja had been arguably the brightest girl in the orphanage where she was raised. It had gotten her knuckles rapped by the nuns for being a smart aleck, and had seen her shunned sometimes by girls who thought she was too smart for her own good.

But she thought she had gotten over the expectation of being the smartest person in the room by about the middle of her first semester as a college freshman. So even if Jadzia was smarter than her by some great yawning gap, it did not follow she had to think herself stupid.

"How would something like that work?" she asked. "Storing energy that way."

Jadzia shrugged. "I am no physicist or engineer, either. But perhaps in some way involv-

ing the molecular bonds of the crystalline structure itself?"

That brought Annja up short. That *did* sound
plausible. At least close enough, given she was
so ignorant of what she'd really need to know to
evaluate the possibility that she didn't even feel
bad about it. She had her own abstruse special-
ties, she reminded herself, and if crystallography
wasn't among them, that was just okay.

"All right," she said, "I'll grant the possibility.
On a purely hypothetical basis. But so what?"

"The scrolls could prove alternate energy
sources were available," Jadzia said, "without
the inefficiencies of wind or solar power, or the
risks of nuclear."

Annja shook her head and laughed. "It's not
as if they contain a set of blueprints for harness-
ing that power."

Jadzia's smile widened until she reminded
Annja forcibly of a cat who'd just discovered
how to work the catch on the birdcage. "But
maybe that's—" she patted the green-and-purple
synthetic bag plumped beside her on the wall
"—still in here."

"SO WHAT DO WE DO NOW?" the young woman asked.

Jadzia sat on a wall again, drumming her heels against it. This time it was a short retaining wall high up on the town's ancient acropolis, looking out over the strip of city lights running along the darkness of the Mediterranean. Above her left shoulder, illuminated by floodlights at the base, rose the shiny red granite obelisk miscalled Pompey's Pillar. Annja knew it was actually built by Diocletian on the ruins of the Temple of Serapis in 297 A.D. Off to her right a smallish sort of Sphinx lay pensive on its pedestal.

Annja paced downslope of her this time, without great energy but still driven. Reaction had set in. They had passed the afternoon wandering in and out of shops in a daze. Annja could remember nothing specific of what they had seen.

They had dinner at a couscous restaurant. Even with ample doses of hot sauce it tasted like wood chips to Annja. They had talked some, sporadically, in muted voices. That was how shock-fatigued they had become. Jadzia was too wasted to be either loud or nasty.

She had told Annja some of her story. She

proudly claimed descent from Mozart, which struck Annja as implausible. To Annja's surprise the girl had been born in the United States, eighteen years before, meaning she carried dual citizenship. Her father, a mathematics professor at the University of Krakow, had been a vocal supporter of the Solidarity labor-union movement. When the Soviet-backed Polish regime had cracked down on Solidarity and arrested its leader, Lech Walesa, Jadzia's father had fled to the U.S. Sobieslaw Arkadczyk moved in with cousins in Chicago and took a job as a plumber.

While there he had met, through friends, a young Polish woman finishing her Ph.D. in economics at the University of Chicago. They had fallen in love and married.

After political reform brought an effective end to the Communist regime, the couple returned to their homeland. With them went their two-year-old daughter, Jadzia. They were soon both teaching at Krakow University. Sobieslaw's having been exiled for supporting Walesa, who became the nation's president in 1990, probably hadn't hurt their opportunities.

Jadzia had shown signs of extraordinary gifts

at a young age. Annja got the impression Sobieslaw and Roksana, Jadzia's mother, were probably looking pretty hard. Parents did that, Annja knew from observing her contemporaries who had produced offspring. She had no direct experience with parents of her own that she could remember.

In Jadzia's case, genius wasn't all in her parents' eyes, it seemed. Tests demonstrated that she had an astonishing facility for languages, as well as a talent for mathematics.

She was, perhaps inevitably, relentlessly indulged from a very early age.

Jadzia learned to read at the advanced age of three. She did so voraciously. As Annja had, she quickly fell in love with the intrigue and adventure and romance of history. That led to a near obsession with ancient languages.

Oddly, she chose not to study specific languages at school. "Why?" Annja asked.

"I learn them perfectly well by myself," she replied matter-of-factly.

Instead she studied linguistics and cryptology,

the better to decipher unknown languages and tantalizing fragments.

As the sun set and Jadzia finished her story, they had drifted up the hill. Wandering the tourist attractions had kept them masked by crowds during the day. They had already checked out of the hotel where they had spent half of last night, and locked their baggage, except for the scrolls, in lockers at the train station. Tonight they would check into a new hotel as late as possible. Hostelries had to report all foreign guests to the police. The later the pair showed their passports, though, the more likely the hotel staff was to wait until morning to pass the information along to the police. And the less likely the police were to actually notice them at all. Just because their pursuers could readily bribe the Alexandrian police didn't mean they could make them efficient.

And now at last Jadzia had asked the question, literally, of life and death: What do we do now?

"We have to find a way to get whoever is hunting us off our backs," Annja answered.

"How can we do that?"

"We could give them what they want."

"Sure," Jadzia sneered. "And then they kill us anyway."

She had gotten so lethargic Annja was almost relieved to see her get snotty again. Almost.

"That's true," she said.

"What? You aren't going to accuse me of conspiracy theories?"

Annja laughed without a lot of humor. "As you pointed out, somebody really is conspiring against us. But what if we were to negate the value of what you're carrying?"

The girl's eyes turned to blue slits of suspicion. "What do you mean?"

"Release the information the scrolls contain," Annja said. "If whoever's after us is willing to kill to keep the information secret, and I confess I can't think of any other reason they attacked you, then it stands to reason that if we make the information public, they'll have no more incentive to kill us. Doesn't it?"

"What if they still want to kill us for revenge?"

Annja shrugged. "It's possible. But murder is an

expensive proposition, even for the rich and well-connected. Continuing a vendetta against a couple of young women—who have incidentally become world-famous figures—might not make a whole lot of sense when vast profit or power no longer lie at stake. Whoever ordered the hit on your dig team, whether it was a corporate executive or government minister, probably has powerful rivals who aren't any more scrupulous than he is. Wasting resources closing the barn door after the horse has escaped might be all the pretext such rivals might need to make a move against him."

She held her breath then, uncertain of whether the girl was going to go off on her or not. She was like nitroglycerin.

But Jadzia smiled, then laughed. "Twisted," she said. "I like the way you think."

And what would worldwide notoriety do for my career? Annja wondered. As an archaeologist, as a consultant for *Chasing History's Monsters*, as champion of good?

She shrugged. A lot less harm than getting abruptly dead in the next few days, she conceded to herself.

"But what about *revenge?*" Jadzia asked.

Annja did not particularly care for the gleam she saw in the young Polish linguist's eyes. In part that was because she wasn't so sure it wasn't shining from her own.

She found herself smiling. "Can you think of anything better," she asked, "than revealing the secret they want so very badly to keep?"

6

"We're still waiting," the fresh-faced Mormon guy said. Although his hair didn't seem to be receding he managed to show a lot of forehead in the late-morning sunlight. His forehead bulged, somehow.

"For what?" Jadzia asked.

Seagulls wheeled over the Bay of Naples in the bright blue morning sky, complaining of fate. The Mediterranean wind stirred the scrubby pines dotted across the hillside and rattled dust and small porous pebbles against larger rocks and randomly rearranged them in clumps at the bases of the wiry plants. The square smelled of dust and ancient dressed stone and not-so-ancient hot asphalt from the parking lot. Annja felt the weight of time and mortality as she and Jadzia walked with their attentive guides through the ruins of Herculaneum.

Which was a familiar and pleasant feeling for the archaeologist.

The two women were being escorted through a ghost town of pallid stone by several researchers from Brigham Young University and a few employees of the small Herculaneum museum, which, like the site as a whole, was closed to the public at the moment. Annja and Jadzia were getting a personal tour as a professional courtesy.

The researchers seemed excited to meet Annja, a genuine television celebrity, and one from their field—one moreover who might somehow be able to bring the manna of airtime or even coveted television-network dollars to their project. But Jadzia they actually seemed to regard with awe. It was as if a rising baseball superstar were visiting another team's locker room.

"For the permission by the Italian government," said Pellegrino. In his early thirties, he was the oldest of the museum crew. He was short and wiry, if a bit bandy-legged. He wore a horizontally striped red-and-blue jersey over shorts. "Further excavation has been held up until the ministry decides whether to give priority to a conservation strategy first."

"Or until the Americans come up with a bigger bribe," said Tancredo, a tall young man with a shock of straw blond hair, blue eyes and a Lombard accent.

The volcano-doomed Roman village perched on the warty flank of the mountain that killed it, alongside the modern village of Ercole. This part of the Bay of Naples was postcard-pretty, and seemingly placid despite the volcano's vast gray dome hulking overhead. But it sported a history almost as long and dense as the land Annja and Jadzia had just left on the other side of the Mediterranean.

"There are legitimate issues at stake!" yelped Tammaro, the third and youngest of the museum crew, who was very short indeed and looked as if he hadn't shaved in three days. The locals had all been speaking Italian. Now Tammaro, stung by the blond northerner's suggestion, bubbled into expostulating in the local dialect, quite different from standard Italian. Annja could barely follow.

The Mormon, whose name was Tom Ross, shrugged. He spoke in English. Still, from his body language Annja guessed he had followed the Italian conversation about as far as she had. He had told the visitors he had done his mission in Italy before returning to Brigham Young University, where he was a graduate student.

"A few of us keep on keeping on here," he said, causing Annja to wonder if this cheerful straight-arrow had any inkling of the phrase's origin in the drug-happy sixties. "The ministry's been promising to get us word 'any time now' since about February." BYU, it seemed, wasn't wasting any full professors on a prospect as tenuous as an Italian ministry doing its job.

Pellegrino scowled and said a word Annja was unfamiliar with. She guessed it was a curse of some sort. Her guess seemed confirmed when Jadzia burst into loud high-pitched giggles. Tammaro hunched his head between his shoul-

ders like a startled turtle and scowled ferociously, an effect somewhat spoiled by the fact
that he also turned beet-red.

They walked through a broad courtyard or
smallish plaza between the stone faces of exca-
vated buildings, some two stories tall. A palm
tree waved badly weathered fronds, half of them
dead and brown, in the insistent breeze. The
empty doorways and windows looked like
openings into skulls, and the sense of desolation
was palpable despite the fact they walked
through what amounted to a very vital modern
city. Maybe it was the sudden and horrid fashion
in which so many lives had been snuffed at once
by one of Mother Nature's better-known disas-
ters.

Or perhaps it was the brooding presence of the
mountain itself, the two-humped saddle shape,
taller Vesuvius separated from ancient Somma
by the Valley of the Giant. The old killer lay
dormant now, although it had smoldered some a
few decades ago.

Annja had studied enough geology to know
that a sleeping volcano could wake quickly. It

had been realized in her own lifetime that extinction wasn't necessarily forever, where volcanoes were concerned. And over four hundred thousand people lay in harm's immediate way if Vesuvius should suddenly take a mind to take up his bad old ways.

"What about equipment to read the scrolls?" Jadzia asked, yanking Annja somewhat guiltily back to the subject pressingly at hand. Merely our own survival, she reflected glumly. "I understood you were going to obtain the equipment to read the carbonized scrolls from the Villa of the Papyri."

"You mean the machines necessary to perform multispectral imaging and CT scans?" Tancredo asked. "Sorry. Hasn't happened yet."

Tom shrugged. "We have an American patron bankrolling much of this operation," he said. "He's real generous. But his generosity sort of hits Pause when it comes to shelling out millions of dollars for an undertaking that might take years before it can actually get started. If ever."

Annja's lips peeled back from her teeth in a grimace. She could feel Jadzia approaching a boil. But neither said anything.

"But it is a most important question," Tammaro said, back to speaking intelligible Italian again, "whether to concentrate our efforts on preserving the ancient treasures of Herculaneum and Lucius Piso's villa, or exploit them for the curiosity and profit of soulless—"

"Oh, put a sock in it, do," Tancredo said in startling English. "It's all about the bribes our wealthy patron can be held up for, and the whole bloody world knows it!'

Pellegrino showed a wavery smile to Annja and Jadzia. "Welcome to Italy," he said.

"WAIT," Annja said, as the taxi rattled down a fairly rural road carved into the cold lava skirts of Vesuvius, where the picturesque gnarled evergreens and palms of the southeastern, seaward side of the mountain gave slow way to stands of alders and birch trees. Their driver, a stout, sweating man with a mustache and a touring cap, had informed them before lapsing into silence that they must detour to avoid some kind of traffic lockup on the main road that ran along the curve of the bay. "You're telling me if I *don't* believe aliens are visiting the Earth in flying saucers then *I'm* buying into a conspiracy theory?"

"Don't be stupid," Jadzia said. That pet phrase as always hit Annja like a slap. "Listen to the words I am saying. The idea that aliens visit Earth is a hoax perpetrated by the government of the United States to keep people in a state of fear so they will docilely allow themselves to be stripped of their liberties. Do you understand me now?"

Annja turned away, frowning, and pretended to watch a broad-winged hawk out her left-hand window, almost immobile as it kited on thermals. She didn't have a ready riposte, she found; the behavior of her country's government certainly did little to dispel the notion it would whip up fake fears in the public for the very reason Jadzia claimed. But Jadzia's style of discourse turned every assertion into personal attack, which actually made it harder to agree with her on such occasions when she did say something sensible. She's like the anti-Dale Carnegie, Annja thought.

"So what do we do now?" Jadzia asked the question they had been avoiding in a flat tone.

Annja looked back. "Good question."

She gave a warning flick of her eyes at the back of the cabdriver's head. He had spoken fractured English when he picked the women up outside the dig site's wire perimeter. Europeans tended to speak a lot more languages than Americans did, especially cabdrivers, and most especially in a locale such as Naples, which had served as a liberty port for ancient Greeks and Phoenicians and every other fleet whose prows had plowed the blue-green furrows of the Mediterranean for the intervening millennia.

"You've got more experience with the… technology than I do," Annja said. "What would you suggest?"

Jadzia turned and stared at her with one brow furrowed and the other raised. "Hello," she said. "Do you think this is a place to be discussing this?"

SINCE THEY'D DECIDED to move on to Herculaneum, Annja had gotten to know her rambunctious charge better. Flight schedules forced them to cool their heels in Alexandria for another day, staying out in public as late as possible, then diving undercover in a new hotel. Annja had attempted to reach Roux but found, as she often did, that he was nowhere to be found when she wanted his advice.

Annja fretted herself half-sick about the possibility she and the girl would be taken aside during the flight-security check at El Nhouza International Airport. In the current environment of unquestioning compliance with supposed security measures, no one would dare to comment at the sight of two foreign women being led to a discreet office in the back. And if they were never seen again, who would be the wiser?

But at least, Annja had thought, as she waited at an Internet café to hear back from her archaeological contacts about visiting Herculaneum, Jadzia has someone to watch out for her.

ANNJA RESISTED THE URGE to snap at Jadzia. You should at least try to act like the responsible adult here, she told herself in irritation.

Annja continued to exert a tyrannical rule over the girl. Her greatest weapon, she had quickly realized, was Jadzia's unexpressed but obvious fear the older woman might simply abandon her. Annja also knew full well that was the one thing she *couldn't* do. But it didn't stop her from ruthlessly exploiting Jadzia's fear of abandonment, and feeling both superior and guilty because of it.

It was hot in the cab and it smelled bad. The driver smelled like garlic and the decay products of one of those body sprays television ads assured American adolescents would make hot women want to crawl on their laps and lick their hair. Annja couldn't imagine anything making her want to lick anyone's hair. And most women she knew agreed with her that what the body sprays mostly brought to mind was toilet disinfectants.

"How stupid," Jadzia was saying, shaking her head and sneering with her arms tightly folded under her breasts. She wore a tight white sleeveless top that emphasized her attributes, and a red skirt so short it attracted way too much attention for Annja's taste.

"Listen," Annja said, "I'm getting tired of hearing that out of you all the time."

"Then quit being so stupid!" Jadzia snapped.

She was trying to think of some appropriate rejoinder, and coming up just as dry as usual, when the driver suddenly slammed the cab to a stop in the middle of the single-lane road. A green slope fell away down to a rocky-bottomed valley at their left. A four-foot granite wall held up a hillside covered with chunks of red-and-black lava rock to the right.

"Why are you stopping here?" Annja asked the driver in Italian.

He turned around and shoved a black Beretta in her face.

7

The driver's beard-fringed mouth opened to reveal some seriously bad teeth and undoubtedly to emit some kind of cliché-riddled bad-guy speech along with tear-gas-like bad breath. Annja had long ago learned that like everybody else, thugs these days got their self-image from the movies. She felt a rush of hot air on her right hand and cheek as the cab's door was yanked open.

I'm just going to give up on taxis altogether, flashed incongruously through her mind. Like a striking adder her right hand flashed out, seized the cabbie's gun hand and twisted it inward against its wrist to point the Beretta at the windshield. It promptly went off, the crack skull-crackingly loud inside the glorified metal box. The sudden thunder startled the cabbie so much he dropped the handgun. It fell into the footwell.

"Help me!" Jadzia screamed as two men in balaclavas dragged her from the cab.

A third, with some kind of submachine gun slung mostly out of sight behind his back, leaned in to seize the bag with the scrolls. A whistling growl of fury and frustration vented from Annja's throat. Letting go of the cabdriver's wrist, she seized the collar of his jacket, more scuff than leather, and flung him forward over his steering wheel. His head smashed right through the windscreen already crazed and weakened by the bullet. He slumped motionless across the wheel. Pink stained the snaggle-tooth fringes of the hole he had made.

The man who was still trying to find a handle on the green-and-purple satchel cursed in German. His words went a ways toward confirming Annja's gut impression that yet again they were being rousted by multinational Eurotrash goons.

Spooked by the deafening gunshot, he jumped back, hauling on the strap of his weapon.

ANNJA HAD ALWAYS ENJOYED certain gifts, which she eventually came to understand were rare, although nothing abnormal.

Whether she learned them or they were simply part of her being, some began to manifest by the time of her earliest memories. From the outset bigger and older girls in the orphanage tried to intimidate her. First, because she was a quiet, skinny child who sought shelter from the prevailing grimness of her surroundings, as well as a sense of rootlessness she would not be able to articulate to herself until her teen years, by almost compulsive devouring of books. Second, because though the sisters found her willful, and some endeavored for years to break that will without success, the older, slower-thinking girls accused her of sucking up to the nuns by always having the right answer in class.

But imposing on the withdrawn little slip of an Annja Creed turned out to be like imposing on an alley cat. When her enemies tried to ambush her on the playground she became a whirling ball of fury. Sheer ferocity, plus an absolutely indomitable refusal ever to acknowledge herself beaten, taught the other girls the wisdom of leaving her alone. As many times as Annja was knocked to the ground, so many times she got back up—always ready to fight.

Her cannier self-defense mentors, when they learned about Annja's youthful encounters, informed her she already had most of what it took to defend oneself successfully—awareness, the ability to think tactically and presence of mind. The SAS veteran who had introduced her to defensive handgun shooting claimed that keeping presence of mind was the strongest indicator of surviving a fight or any other crisis.

The mental parts—what she had always had to an unusual degree—were what really counted. The rest was technique. Granted, physical skills might well make the difference between living and dying. But without those vital mental attributes, even the most physically formidable, expensively trained and fabulously armed man could be caught off guard and killed with remarkable ease. Annja had seen that for herself more than once, since her destiny had come upon her.

AND NOW IT WAS that ability to keep cool, to retain her presence of mind instead of falling into helpless panic or flailing-blind anger, that kept Annja alive in the killzone of a lethal and well-laid trap.

Annja dived over the seats. For a heart-stopping moment she fumbled around, the sunlight streaming in the open door seeming to dazzle her eyes rather than aid sight. At last her hand closed around the black rubber grips of the driver's fallen Beretta. She flopped onto the backseat with her back against the left-hand door and brought the pistol up one-handed.

The guy in the balaclava had his hands on the fore-and-aft pistol grips of a Beretta submachine gun. As the barrel rose to blast her, Annja made her eyes focus on the foresight of her own weapon. She pointed it at the center of the dark silhouette against all that Mediterranean sunlight and squeezed off two quick shots.

The man jerked to the impacts but did not go down. Body armor! flashed across Annja's mind. Her left hand found her right, wrapped around the fingers to steady her Beretta in an improvised firing position. As the submachine gun's briefly interrupted upward progress resumed, she made her own firearm line up the dark bulb of head like a pumpkin on the post of her front sight.

She squeezed the trigger again. The Beretta rocked in her hand. The head jerked. Pink mist sprayed out into brilliant sunshine. The man dropped instantly.

Impacts filled the cab with jackhammer clamor. It sounded like a hailstorm in the middle of Kansas. Since the sky had barely a cloud to its name and this wasn't Kansas, Annja reasonably reached the flash conclusion it was bullets, not hail. Somebody outside her field of vision was conducting reconnaissance-by-fire on the cab. Or, basically, just shooting the hell out of it in hopes of hitting her.

Jadzia was being dragged up the slope. She wasn't going peacefully. Annja saw the blond girl catch the man on her right with a brutal kick to his shin. It didn't hit right to pop the knee. He backhanded her savagely for her pains.

The cab shook with more bullet strikes. Annja was out of time with no way to help her charge. She twisted in the seat, kicked at her door with both legs. With a squeal of metal, it popped not just the lock but its rusted hinges, and flew clean off the car. It landed on the white roadside gravel with a thump.

Annja was already diving out of the car as bullets stitched the seat. Emerging into the noonday sun she registered two more attackers not twenty feet downslope. They aimed machine pistols at her but didn't fire. From the width of the eyes behind the holes in their face masks, the sight of the rear-left door exploding clean off the taxicab had momentarily paralyzed both of them.

Unfortunately Annja's forward momentum was not going to let her get a shot at them. She opened her hand and let the Beretta fall. As she tucked her head and shoulder for a forward roll she half closed her hand and reached with her mind—

She took the first fall on her left shoulder and rolled through.

As she came up she took hold with her left hand the hilt of the sword that had appeared in her right. The sword that had once belonged to Joan of Arc now belonged to her. Though it rested in some *otherwhere* she couldn't truly understand, she could summon it at will and was growing more confident using it.

The mystic blade caught the first gunman at the waist. Driven by Annja's powerful muscles it cut through cloth, skin, fat and muscle as if through soft cheese. When it struck his spine she felt a jar of resistance.

Annja turned, straightening her right leg to brake her forward progress and drive her into a pivot left to attack the other gunman. She pulled the blade with her. The first gunman jackknifed at the impact of the blade against his midsection.

The second attacker had wits enough about him to turn toward her. She brought the sword around and over her right shoulder. The masked gunman raised his weapon. She had the quick impression it was in an attempt to ward off the sword stroke, not to shoot.

She cut him transversely, right down to left. Continuing the stroke up and around, she cut him again left to right as if completing a giant *X*. He screamed—his partner must have screamed, too, but Annja never heard—then fell.

She glanced around and had to gulp air to keep from losing her breakfast.

Apparently expecting little resistance from a pair of pampered young middle-class women, the two assassins evidently hadn't bothered with hot, cumbersome body armor. The coroner is not going to like that, she thought.

The sudden roar of rotors made her look up. A blue helicopter with white trim swooped overhead, lashing Annja with a horizontal storm of grit and debris. For a moment she felt exhilarating relief—the police!

Then the chopper settled down to a precarious flat spot on a slope fifty yards above the road cut. The other two masked men dragged Jadzia, still kicking and shrieking obscenities, toward it.

Annja took the obscenities on faith. She could no longer hear Jadzia for the beat of the feathered blades. She felt a surge of admiration for the pigtailed blond girl. She wasn't fighting effectually, but by God she was fighting.

One of her abductors swung up an Uzi one-handed and let off a burst at Annja. Most of it hit the taxi with a sound like a woodpecker going after a derelict washing machine. But enough bullets bit chunks out of the sod and kicked up sprays of the crushed gravel lining the roadbed that Annja had to dive and roll uphill for the dubious shelter of the shot-up car. She aimed for the front, where the engine block could pretty reliably be counted on to stop fast-jacketed 9 mm bullets that would slice right through the thin-gauge body of the car.

When she peeked over the hood, the helicopter was rising against the great gray mound of Vesuvius. Jadzia struggled against various sets of restraining arms in the helicopter's open doorway.

No other attackers remained in sight. Annja realized she had never seen whoever had opened fire on the cab first. Evidently that gunman or men had also piled into the aircraft, probably from the other side.

The driver's Beretta still lay where she'd dropped it. Seizing it, Annja snapped to her feet and bounded up the slope like a deer, holding the handgun out before her like a probe. Her long chestnut hair had come loose from the ponytail she kept it pulled into on most occasions. It flew behind her.

She pointed the Beretta at the streamlined hump on the aircraft's back from which the rotor shaft sprang, knowing that was the weakness of any helicopter.

I can hit it, she thought. She had actually downed a helicopter once by throwing a grappling hook on a nylon line into the rotor circle and fouling the blades. Think what I can do with an actual weapon.

She did. And stopped, panting, and lowered the handgun.

I could shoot the chopper down, she realized, with Jadzia inside.

Across two hundred yards the girl's bright blue eyes caught Annja's as the helicopter sucked its landing gear up into its sleek belly. And though the sound of her voice had no hope of carrying past the noise of twin turbine engines and great sweeping rotor blades, her mouth unmistakably formed the words, "Help me."

"I will!" Annja shouted back, brandishing the pistol.

The chopper soared up and away to the northwest across the stunning blue sky.

8

A hood was yanked unceremoniously over Jadzia Arkadczyk's pigtails. She was thrust emphatically into a seat. Her wrists were yanked together before her and a plastic restraint twisted around them. A gruff Italian-accented voice told her in English she should sit there and not cause trouble, or she would regret it.

She sat and did not cause trouble. She regretted it anyway.

She wept. Hysterically at first. Then as she got tired, she subsided into whimpering. That in turn dwindled as she got control of herself and she realized it wasn't doing any good and it was making the sack enclosing her head wet and hard to breathe through.

By the time she got that all sorted out in her head the helicopter had touched down. Hard hands hustled her out into the afternoon heat. The pavement beneath the soles of her Converse All-Star knockoffs was so hot she could feel it through the cheap rubber. When she left the circle of ominous sounds made by the idling rotor blades she was unsurprised to hear rising around her a screaming hurricane roar from a horde of jet engines.

A few stumbling steps and she was being half dragged, half pushed up stairs that rang metallic beneath her feet. Jadzia didn't even dare hope someone would spot her, an obvious victim, being hustled aboard some kind of private jet. Likely this was a secluded hangar at Naples airport, probably belonging to her abductor—could it be any other than one or another Satanic limb of Big Oil?—where no one would see.

Even if anyone saw, this was Italy, land of the red Brigades and the Mafia, and more particularly Naples, which, like Marseilles, boasted a record of piratical skullduggery dating back to approximately the dawn of writing. Anyone who spotted her being kidnapped would simply pass it off as business as usual.

"Dude? What the fuck?" an American-accented voice asked from up the ramp.

"Ran into some problems," the guy pushing her up on her left said with a French accent. "Change of plans."

"Dude! We're supposed to take delivery of, like, two chicks and a bag."

"Shut up!" rapped a German voice, apparently from the guy who was towing Jadzia up the ramp by her right biceps. "We speak more inside."

She hit a barrier of cool air and was swallowed within. A new hand took her right arm. The French guy released her left. The new hand urged her back and into a comfortable chair. As muffled sounds of argument came from the front of the aircraft she was buckled in. Immediately the engine scream began to rise to a piercing mosquito whine.

Jadzia felt a stab of optimism. Maybe it's a

Gulf stream, she thought. She had always wanted to ride in a Gulf stream, a big expensive executive jet she had often read about in Tom Clancy novels.

The airplane taxied for a time then took off. Some time later the dark cloth hood was removed. When her vision coalesced from random fields of fuzz, there in the middle of it was a narrow, handsome young Asian face, crinkled slightly with concern.

"You okay?" the man asked in American-accented English. "They didn't, like, hurt you or anything?"

Jadzia had already determined to change her angle of attack. Physical resistance was clearly not going to work. So she blinked her big cornflower-blue eyes at him and gave him her most seductive smile.

He turned and fled toward the front of the aircraft.

"WHAT IS THE MATTER, Lee?" the lanky Russian asked. "You look as if you have just seen ghost."

"That girl," the Asian kid said. "She, like, smiled at me."

The Russian cocked a ginger-colored eyebrow. "So? You may look but not touch. Or Gus Marshall takes your man-junk off with belt sander, maybe." He laughed and laughed as if this were the greatest joke of all.

Lee shook his head emphatically, whipping his luxurious ponytail around his shoulders. "No, man. She's totally hot. But the way she looked at me—I'd rather hook up with a barracuda. You can see it in her eyes. She's scary crazy, man."

"Is slang?" the Russian asked.

"What?" Lee asked blankly. "No, man. It's slang for she's, like, Angelina-Jolie-in-her-Billy-Bob-Thornton-phase crazy. Drink-each-other's-blood crazy."

"Oh," the Russian said, slightly crestfallen. "I guess is not good."

HER ATTEMPT at gaining the cooperation of her captors through her seductive wiles having failed miserably, Jadzia sulked for hours, refusing food or drink, as the airplane flew north. Then the organism made its demands known. She started screaming for attention.

A tall, goony-looking guy with prominent ears and a bad ginger crewcut came loping down the aisle in response. He wouldn't meet her eyes and seemed to be sweating. She knew the look and addressed him in peremptory Russian.

He unbuckled her from her seat and escorted her to a dark-stained walnut-paneled door.

"Untie my hands," she commanded in the haughty tone appropriate to a proud Pole addressing a Russian lout.

He turned and called a nervous query in English.

"So cut her loose, idiot," came a command through a closed curtain.

"No-culture German fascist," the Russian muttered in his own language as he produced a blade to cut the plastic restraint.

The bathroom was comparatively large and luxuriously appointed in brushed brass and cream tones. She was fairly sure now this really was a Gulf stream. She took her time and used the privacy to think about ways to disable the aircraft. Some ideas promptly came to her quick, capacious mind.

And were just as promptly dismissed. She

was, it occurred to her, *flying* in said aircraft. Disabling it suddenly seemed like not such a hot idea. She wasn't ready to admit these clowns had gotten the better of her, the certified girl genius.

Thinking about Annja calmed her. Annoying though she was, the woman did show remarkable abilities. She was almost like a real-life version of her favorite adventure-novel heroines.

More to the point, she seemed to have decided she was personally responsible for Jadzia's welfare. And though she was maybe not as bright as Jadzia—but then, who was?—she did seem the sort to take her responsibilities seriously.

Jadzia decided to allow the plane to continue on its flight. She would return to her seat and make the jug-eared Russian bring her the food and drink she had been promised earlier. And she would rely on the mysterious Ms. Creed to come to rescue her.

THE GULF STREAM FLEW out over a sizable body of water. It was either the Baltic or the North Sea, Jadzia knew, pretty much by default. The spring day, short at such northerly latitudes, was already ending in a pool of fire out the port-side windows, and gilt clouds of gray and lavender velvet out the starboard side where Jadzia sat.

Almost apologetically, the handsome American Asian in the dark suit and the Russian in the yellow polyester shirt and faded dungarees came back to hood her again.

As they tried to pull the bag over her head, without conscious decision, Jadzia abandoned her strategy of cooperation and started screaming. She didn't target the Asian kid particularly, because he was actually quite cute, which convinced her he couldn't be all bad. But she nailed the Russian in the crotch with a rising instep that lifted him up a good inch, caused his little watery blue boar eyes to bug out and his ears to burn red as he doubled over.

The Asian kid was fast as a rattler. He took advantage of Jadzia's reflexive pause in frantic activity to admire the effect her kick hit had on the Russian—she'd never actually kicked anyone in the nuts before—to whip the hood right over her head. Unable to target effectively, she felt her wrists seized and strapped together again with a nasty plastic strip that bit into her skin when she fought against it.

She cursed her captors enthusiastically in several languages.

Her oppressors fled.

She settled back to sulk some more.

When the aircraft touched down, someone unsnapped her from her seat, urged her up and guided her forward along the aisle to the front of the aircraft, then out into a brisk, saltwater-scented breeze.

She stayed on autopilot and let the world happen around her. It wasn't as if she was unaccustomed to zoning out into a private world of intellectual reverie.

She was escorted across the apron and handed into a new craft. When the engines spun up with a turbine whine and unmistakable chop she knew it for another helicopter. It leaped in the air, angled, and was away.

How long it flew she didn't try to track. From a general impression of light through the cloth hood and decreasing temperature she gathered the sun was setting.

The chopper rose, then settled to a landing. Still hooded and with her wrists still bound before her, she was unstrapped from the seat and gently but insistently urged out of the aircraft.

Cold spray-freighted wind struck her like a slap. She was led at a brisk pace into clammy darkness, up echoing metal stairs.

She knew where she was.

Not specifically. But she knew quite well what kind of place it was.

The question that rang in her mind, was, How will Annja Creed find me here?

9

As soon as Annja's eyes adjusted to the tavern's gloom, her heart plummeted straight to the soles of her shoes.

The man she had come to Germany to seek out was here, all right, just as she'd been told. He sat behind a rampart of empty upturned one-liter beer steins like some kind of ancient monolith. Totally hammerheaded drunk.

It was a cozy tavern outside a cozy little village in a cozy little valley tributary to the Rhine near the city of Darmstadt in Hessen. The setting was quite bucolic, complete with its castle on an overlording hilltop. It all oozed *picturesque*.

Across from Annja's target a young local in a wool sweater sat hunched slightly forward beneath the square roof timbers that hung dark and low. He had rumpled brown hair and round-rimmed spectacles and looked fourteen at the way outside. He smiled dreamily across his own set of upturned steins at Annja's quarry. They looked as if they were playing megalithic chess.

"Your turn," the young man said in English. His lips were loose and moist.

The other blinked at him. He pushed his trademark white Stetson cowboy hat back on his lank blond hair. "You're on, partner," he said in a broad Western American drawl.

A last stein stood in the middle of the table between them. It was filled with a liquid that looked amber in the doubtful light. He reached for it. His hand trembled. He looked at it with bright blue eyes and frowned. The hand stopped trembling.

He picked up the big mug.

The tavern had burbled with conversation and barked with mirth. Now it fell still, except for the odd creak and scrape of a table leg on the floor and a loud, fruity belch, quickly stifled. The locals were crowded behind the German kid to egg him on. By the bar behind the man in the hat a bunch of Americans and Canadians stood, with one or two Brits evident among them by their accents. These seemed mostly crew for the show *Past Master,* a stablemate of Annja's own *Chasing History's Monsters,* which had just wrapped up shooting. The castle by the village enjoyed a certain notoriety, Annja knew, for all the wrong reasons.

The man in the hat had come to help clear up that confusion. His name was Tex Winston and he was the program's star and guiding light. Although she had never met him, rumor around the network claimed he was a real-life adventurer, not just a television special effect. Of course, Annja was skeptical. She knew the claims the network publicity department made about her.

He *looked* the part, she had to admit. He was tall, tanned, blond and lanky. But she had known most of that from seeing him on the tube. Except for the tall part, since a great many TV and movie personalities, she knew from firsthand observation, were surprisingly short. He could do anything, rumor said—had done everything, twice. He knew everybody worth knowing on both sides of every ocean and every law. It was whispered he had served as a U.S. Army Ranger, had seen action in Central America, Africa and the Far East.

She hoped the stories were true. Because Annja looked on him as, just possibly, her one and only hope.

It rankled her beyond belief to have to throw herself upon the good graces of a stranger—to have to ask this man for help, she who had always been so self-sufficient. But more lay at stake than her pride, or even her life. Somewhere out in that night a vulnerable young girl was lost and afraid and alone. Annja knew she was all the hope Jadzia had.

With a big old Texas smile Winston sat back. Confidently he raised the glass mug to his lips. He tipped his head back and chugged the dense local brew with startling alacrity. He lowered the mug to the table with an authoritative thump and wiped his mouth with the back of his hand.

He then fell face forward onto the table with a thump and a crash of upset beer steins, and emitted a wood-rasp snore.

The Germans went crazy, shouting and clapping their young champion on his narrow shoulders. He blinked at them as if unsure to which species they belonged. A short, skinny, bandy-legged crew member with a shaved, tattooed head and three rings in his right ear moved hastily to Tex Winston's side, possibly to see if he was still alive.

A short and stout local with a bristling black mustache and a fuzzy green vest turned from the black-stained oak bar at Annja's elbow and thrust a full stein into her hand.

"Welcome to Frankenstein, Fräulein Annja Creed," he said.

TEX WINSTON SANG in a clear but fairly tone-deaf tenor voice.

"Come on," Annja said, half under her breath, half to the man whose arm she had wound around her shoulder. He was taller than she was, and despite the relaxation induced by alcohol and conviviality the arm felt like steel cable wrapped around rebar, and the body slumped against hers was as firm as a well-packed bag of cement. If she hadn't been in a state of internal warfare between being disconsolate and really pissed off, it might have been interesting. Instead she urged him along through the dark with the roadbed cinder crunching beneath their feet. "Walk it off," she said.

The old-fashioned tavern sign clapped behind them in the wind like a wooden bell. A big square head was painted on it, complexion greenish in the light from a streetlight up the narrow country lane. Stitches spread across its forehead and a bolt stuck out of its neck like a piercing gone terribly awry.

From the respectful attention the assembled crowd had given Tex Winston as she steered him up the short tavern steps and out into the coolly humid night, he was pretty popular with locals and crew. That, at least, was a good sign. In Annja's experience the way people treated you when you were drunk showed how they really felt about you.

But the tavern-goers' attitude had annoyed her, as well. Everybody seemed to recognize her, too, from her own show. And they all seemed to think Tex had just gotten really lucky.

She attributed that to her mild celebrity. When she looked in the mirror Annja didn't see the tall, lean, leggy and drop-dead gorgeous woman, her chestnut hair that could never stay restrained, challenging amber-green eyes, and face whose length and strong cheekbones all contributed to a striking appearance. In her own eyes Annja was eternally the gawky adolescent with the ridiculously long stick legs and all the grace of a new-born foal who had yet to get the hang of walking.

"'S *wrong,* you know," Winston told her, letting his head loll on his neck, gesturing vaguely back toward the tavern. The road bent left into shadow, winding its way between green fields and darkly forested hills. Ahead of them the tower of the infamous castle rose above the trees. "The sign. *That's* not the monster. Oh, no. Not the real monster of Frankenstein. Just something Hollywood made up outta Mary Shelley's book."

"I do know," Annja said. She wasn't feeling too indulgent.

He looked at her again, squeezing his brows over his pale blue eyes with such cartoon-intense scrutiny Annja couldn't help laughing aloud.

"Thassright," he said. "You're Annja Creed. You know a thing or two about monsters. You tracked down that critter in France."

"The Beast of Gevaudan," she said, grimacing slightly.

"Yeah. So I'm preachin' to the choir here, aren't I? You prolly know the real story."

She nodded. "A knight returning from the Crusades found an ogre, or possibly a dragon, terrorizing the villagers," she said. "He slew it and was ennobled as Baron von Frankenstein, and given the village as a fief. Keep moving."

He nodded loopily. "Closhe enough." He was a sloppy drunk, but fortunately an amiable one. He had a reputation for being a genuinely nice guy—which in the entertainment world either meant oceans or nothing at all. "Tavern name is Monster's Cellar. But they got the wrong monster."

"That figures," she said.

He laughed, head bobbing again. Then he stopped and turned a worried frown to her.

"What are you doing here, anyway?" His eyes narrowed. "This isn't some stunt dreamed up by those network flacks, is it?"

"I need your help," she said.

His gaze slid past her. Suddenly his eyes went wide. He shoved her away from him hard.

The hardwood club swished down between them, cleaving the space her skull had occupied an instant before.

10

The club-wielder cursed. As he tried to recover, Annja snapped a backfist around into his face. He sat down hard in the road.

A wheel of movement drew Annja's eyes back to Winston in time to see him bending forward with a pair of somebody else's legs sticking straight up in the air above him. The inebriated show host tucked the man's shaved head against his own chest as he carried through with his shoulder throw. The man slammed down on his back in the road with an impact Annja felt. She heard an explosion of breath.

Winston straightened. He looked around. His

manner was alert, elastic; the loosy-goosy drunkenness of a few heartbeats before had snapped as taut as if it had never been. Annja saw a flicker of motion right behind him, heard a nasty crack. He dropped to his knees, moaning and grabbing for the back of his head with both hands.

Annja took two running steps, leaped over the kneeling Winston, and dealt a flying side kick to the man who had clubbed him from behind. She caught the man in the sternum as he raised his ax handle for a swing at her. She felt bone give beneath her heel, heard a sound like a pistol shot as ribs broke. The man flew backward into darkness.

Annja landed easily on her feet. Instantly two more black-clad men rushed her from right and left. She turned to her right, jumped straight up. Her right leg shot out in a front kick, her left straight back. She felt two impacts, heard two grunts as her assailants were knocked back by her double kick.

She heard the man behind her land on his butt on the gravel. The attacker to her front reeled back but kept his feet. She skipped forward, launched a front snap kick into his solar plexus. He doubled over. She stepped into him, driving a palm-heel uppercut up under his chin with her right hand.

A fist thudded against the side of her jaw and threw her to the ground.

But one of the strengths of her boxing training was learning to take a punch as well as deliver one. Though she sprawled gracelessly on the ground she rolled sideways by reflex. By the time she came up into a low three-point crouch she was mostly recovered. The whole right side of her face felt as if it had been anesthetized, but she didn't think her jaw was broken.

A wiry shaved-headed man in black jeans, running shoes and a pullover faced her, bouncing on the balls of his feet, fists up. "Your fancy kicks won't work on me, bitch," he said.

She sensed others closing in on her from three sides. Nonetheless she focused a brief glare on him. "I am so tired of guys calling me that," she said.

She sprang into a forward rolling handstand. The nun who had taught her gymnastics would have made her do ten pushups for the sloppiness of her form. Especially the way the heel of her right foot shot out and came slamming down on her opponent's exposed forehead.

He dropped like a slaughtered steer. They didn't call that an ax kick for nothing, she thought.

She sprang onto her feet. Her head was clear despite the packed-in-cotton-batting sensation that filled half her face. In her peripheral vision she caught a figure closing from her left, raising a stick of some kind, and another lunging toward her from the right.

A forearm snaked out of the darkness around the throat of the club wielder. It was a wiry, tanned forearm, mostly exposed by a blue denim sleeve rolled three-quarters up it. For some reason her eyes registered the little golden hairs on the arm, gleaming in the streetlight. A hand clasped the forearm's wrist, locking it around her assailant's neck.

She wheeled left. An ax handle whistled down at her face. She whipped her right foot up in a crescent kick that caught the stick's flat side with the inner curve of her shoe and torqued it right out of the wielder's hands.

He cursed. The hardwood stung his palms as it twisted free. He recovered rapidly, though, fired a fast looping haymaker at her face with his right fist. She leaned her torso back and left. The fist swished harmlessly by. He closed with a straight left. She brought up her right forearm, hand open, and simply wedged the blow harmlessly past her head.

Left foot advanced, he came around with a right cross, surprisingly well delivered considering the barroom sloppiness of his opening punch. She turned into it, widdershins, bringing up her left forearm to contact the inside of his right forearm and help steer it by. Then she wheeled around with a right backfist right above the eyes.

She was in control now. The blow forced the man to cross his eyes and take a jelly-leg step back. She turned her torso left, rolled her hips, cocked her right leg and kicked straight back.

Her heel hit him right between belt and crotch. A shot like that, to the hypogastric region, would trip the body's neural circuits, though nowhere so completely as a good solar-plexus or groin shot—although more reliably than the latter. Annja also knew that the movies notwithstanding, about one guy in four is invulnerable to a blow to the family jewels. What that said for the male of the species she wasn't sure, but her concern was primarily tactical.

The kick was mainly aimed at blasting his pelvis right out from below his center of mass. As go the hipbones, so goes everything, she thought. It worked. His body went perfectly horizontal and dropped right down on the hard-packed road shoulder. His chin bounced with a nasty crack. It might've broken, and for that matter she might have cracked his pelvis with the kick. She didn't care. Her concern was not to kill if it wasn't necessary. She hadn't.

She came smartly around, ready for action. She heard the slap of running soles, some crunching in crushed gravel, others like fading applause on asphalt. Their assailants were fleeing, leaving three of their number lying in Annja's view.

Tex Winston stood nearby brushing grit from various lanky parts of his person. He gave her a grin.

Then he turned away, doubling over and grabbing his knees.

"Tex?" She took a worried step toward him.

He waved her off. "Don't worry," he said, digging with his other hand in a pocket of his jeans. He sounded breathless, constricted, and a slight whistle ran like a thread through his words. "I know better'n to stand like this when I can't breathe. Doesn't help a bit."

He straightened. His shoulders were heaving. He brought something small that flashed white in the streetlight up to his mouth. She heard a hiss, followed by a shuddering inhalation. He stood straight with obvious effort, holding his breath for a long interval. Then he exhaled in a way that made him seem to lose an inch of height, took two deliberate breaths and gave a shaky smile.

"Fighting always gives me asthma," he said. "Good a reason as any to try to avoid it, I reckon."

"Thanks for your help," she said.

"Didn't look like you needed much," he said. "Not many men could've handled themselves half so well, lady, and I've seen some real pros in action."

She forced free a self-deprecating laugh. "They underestimated me because I'm a woman."

"Sure," he said. He bent down, recovered his Stetson, batted it against the fanny of his jeans to get the grit off it.

"I got lucky."

"Anything you say, ma'am." He settled the hat on his short blond hair with a certain care.

She gave up and started examining the casualties. The three she could see were all breathing, which was a relief for reasons she couldn't quite touch at the moment.

"Ms. Creed," Tex Winston said, "one thing's sure—you don't believe in fighting fair." He shook his head, but his voice held a note of admiration.

"I don't believe in fighting *unnecessarily,*" she said. "If it's worth fighting for, it's worth winning." She looked around. So far it didn't seem their ruckus had attracted much attention.

"I wonder why they didn't use guns," she said before she caught herself. From the corner of her eye she saw Tex raise an eyebrow. He said nothing. Pretty eloquently, she thought.

One of the fallen groaned and tried to sit up. He had sandy hair and a pale freckled face, both greenish in the streetlight, and maybe for other reasons, as well. He wore a beard of blood that ran down his throat and blended into his black turtleneck.

"Ooh," he moaned. "You busted my bloody *teef.*" He spoke with a distinctive Cockney accent.

His eyes focused on her as Annja bent down over him. "You *bi*—"

She grabbed the front of his pullover. It was wet and sticky. It still creeped her out a bit, although it was hardly an unfamiliar sensation at this stage of her life. "Don't say it," she snapped, as she hoisted his upper torso off the grit and cocked a fist.

He winced and shut up.

"Who sent you?" she asked. "Why?"

He laughed. It was a ghastly bloody bubble,

a blood spring around jagged yellowish stubs. "Why? Are you bloody thick, woman? For the scrolls. And you. What do you think?"

"Who?" she repeated. "Talk."

He laughed again. She cocked the fist farther back. He just laughed louder.

Somewhere off in the night a siren began its warble.

"Come on," Tex suggested softly. "The German cops haven't got much sense of humor, you probably know. He's won this round."

Annja looked from Tex back to the Brit thug. She glared down at him. The laughter stopped and his eyes widened.

She let him fall back with a thud.

"Okay," Tex Winston said, his eyes like big blue saucers in the light of the bedside table lamp. "So. You got yourself a magic sword that follows you around in its own little bubble universe."

He essayed a laugh and found it small and shaky.

They sat in his surprisingly modest hotel room outside the village. Annja was cross-legged on his bed, while he sat in a chair by the radiator beneath the window. Each had a can of chilled fruit juice bought from a dispenser. She was glad he hadn't decided to resume drinking beer.

"What does that mean, exactly?" he asked. His expression was unreadable by the half light of a table lamp dialed low.

"I was afraid you'd ask me that. I wish I knew. The sword didn't exactly come with an instruction manual."

He sucked in a deep breath and let it out in a lengthy exhalation. "Whoo. Just my luck to get paired with an apprentice superheroine."

She had risked a trip back to her hotel room to collect the scrolls and her personal effects. She had been terrified the gym bag had been stolen. It was the key to Jadzia's safety. Once the bad guys got hold of it, the girl's survival became purely optional.

Tex kept watch outside. When she came out he said nobody seemed to be spying on her, and nobody followed them back to his own hotel room. She tended to believe him. There was a quiet surety to his words, just as to his actions. She'd decided it was worth the risk to tell him about the sword.

He also acted totally sober. Apparently getting jumped was an effective cure for inebriation. She doubted it would catch on.

"Why show me all this?" he asked.

"I need to trust you."

"You must be pretty desperate."

"Believe me," she said, "I am. And I need you to trust me." She sighed a bit raggedly. "Also, the next time we get into a tight place—and if you agree to help me with this, we will, I can pretty much assure you—I might have to use the sword. And if it took you by surprise, the distraction could get you killed."

He looked at her for a few heartbeats in the gloom. His eyebrows slowly rose. "Whooee," he said at length. "You must surely be into something serious."

She told him. She saw no reason not to, and plenty of reason to do so. She did gloss over Jadzia's speculations as to who was after the scrolls, and why.

"Somebody must want those scrolls pretty badly," Tex said, but he didn't press for details.

"Whoever is after us," she said, "obviously has some pretty serious resources."

"And seriously few scruples." He didn't seem particularly alarmed.

"Which makes me wonder all over again—" She pushed a lock of hair from her eyes. Despite the fact it was cool in the room she found herself sweating lightly. "Why didn't this bunch use guns?"

"Lots of possible reasons," Tex said. "They may not have had time to get their first team on you here. Even people like the ones who're after you have limits to their resources. They tend to have to fight a lot of brushfires. And anyway, the Germans tend to take things pretty darn seriously. You start flashing suppressed MP-5s, even if they are a local product, they're liable to drop their antiterrorist unit on your head like a big old sledgehammer. No matter who you are, and I seriously mean, no matter. The Germans may go along with all kinds of dodgy stuff in the name of fighting terror, but they're mighty territorial.

You go poaching on their turf, and there is no such thing as being too big and bad and influential for them to make an example of you."

Annja realized her eyes had gotten wide.

"Doesn't mean we can get complacent," he said. "If the bad guys feel confident enough, or desperate enough, they'll likely just take their chances. And if they are connected enough and smart and mean enough to do—well, what they've done—it's not entirely beyond the realm of possibility they can come around and convince the Germans that we're terrorists."

Annja felt as if she'd swallowed a frozen cantaloupe. "Do you think they will?"

He shrugged. "No telling. My gut tells me they won't. For all the noise that gets made about everybody fighting a global war on terror together there's no such thing as a no-questions-asked op like that. German intelligence will have plenty of questions. And they're not boys 'n girls who like to stop before they got themselves some answers. If that wasn't a concern for whoever's after you, frankly, y'all would be dead already. You and this poor little geek kid both. But you need to be aware of the possibility."

He sat back in his chair. "So why didn't you just whip out your magic sword and bisect a few of those yahoos back there?" he asked. "Was it just because they didn't show guns?"

"It's…complicated. I don't have much trouble killing in self-defense. Or in defense of innocence. And it seems to me if I kill somebody who's attacking me or some innocent person, I'm not just saving myself or even the innocent person, but my attacker's next victim, and the one after that. But still—" she scrunched her cheeks up under her eyes and shook her head.

"My old tae kwon do instructor used to say it was a misuse of TKD *not* to destroy someone who was aggressing against you," Tex said, "for pretty much the same reason. It was part of the student oath we always recited at the beginning of class, to never misuse the art."

He just looked at her. After a moment she sighed and said, "Okay. This is something I have to work out for myself. But I need to take it as it comes to me, I guess. I don't think there are any easy answers."

He looked at her a moment more, though the expression in his blue eyes was unreadable. Then he made a sound down in his throat, which may have been a piece of laughter, and nodded his head once.

"If I'm dealing with somebody who doesn't want it to get too easy to kill people, no matter how good the reason," he said, "reckon I can live with that. Lot easier than the alternative."

ANNJA SAT cross-legged on the bed of her new room, a few doors down from Tex's, with her laptop open before her. Much of the *Past Master* production crew had headed home already, freeing several rooms on the floor of the three-story inn. She had just taken a much-needed and highly restorative shower. She wore a white bathrobe indifferently belted about her and a towel wound around her hair.

She was checking her e-mail. It was her lifeline, like everybody else's, and more reliable than her cell phone despite the fact coverage was getting near to being truly global. One thing Roux had actually deigned to teach her—her life was going to go on, sword or not. As long as she lived she would have the same concerns and bear the same burdens as any everyday person, along with the weight of her destiny.

Her mail reassured her by its very mundanity.

As she scrolled down her features twisted in brief annoyance. A spam message had escaped her software filters. Worse, it was a blindingly obvious scam, judging from the header, which read, "Your Urgent Attention Required."

"I'm gonna have to check my filters again," she muttered darkly. She poised a finger above the delete key.

And froze.

The sender was *Jadzia*.

"'DEARLY BELOVED, in the name of Our Lord Jesus Christ I greet you.'"

Dressed in jeans and his unbuttoned denim cowboy shirt, Tex Winston sat on the edge of his bed reading aloud from the screen of Annja's computer, which sat opened on his knees. Annja knelt on the bed behind him looking over his shoulder. She wore a T-shirt and a pair of jeans. Her feet were bare.

She was finding it harder than she expected not to think about the rock-ribbed torso shadowed inside the open shirt, even if it wasn't currently in her field of vision. Maybe surviving danger really did bring on a life-affirming response. She was both tired and wired, a combination she knew to be dangerous in all ways, and anyway she hardly knew him, she told herself.

"I am Sakimi Taylor, wife of the recently deposed president of Liberia, Charles Taylor… You must reply within forty-eight hours in order to guarantee delivery of certain materials. Otherwise my daughter, who is a mathematical prodigy of some note, faces death from the Liberian rebels who have captured her."

Tex looked over his shoulder at Annja. "Give the devil his due," he said with half a grin, "this is genius."

"Forgive me if I don't appreciate it too much," Annja said, frowning.

He shook his head. "Sorry. Don't mean to be flip. But this shows some imagination."

"But it might've been caught by my filters," she said. "Plus I almost deleted it unread."

"Well—" he shrugged "—it worked. And that's pretty much the only real signpost we have in this bad old world. If you're the sort of person who only thinks about results."

She gathered that, while he was good at thinking about results, and getting them, he was no more inclined to think only in terms of them than she was. *Unless he's just another clever scammer.*

Yet she had no choice but to trust him.

"What do we do now?" She struggled to keep the fear she felt from showing in her eyes or voice.

Perhaps by happenstance he looked back at the screen. "Go to sleep," he said.

"What?"

"Did you ever know anything to get better 'cause you lost sleep over it? We're gonna need to be frosty these next forty-eight hours. Mighty frosty."

Annja sighed and got up off the bed. "What then?"

He grinned at her. "We are going to need some serious nerdage," he said. He stretched and yawned. "Fortunately, ol' Tex knows just where to find us some."

11

The room was dim and smelled like old socks and mildew. There were pizza boxes strewed about the floor. It was small and crowded with a rumpled, unmade bed and a couple of ratty chairs and racks of electronic equipment of mysterious and ominous purpose.

Nothing says Germany like delivery pizza, Annja thought. But I guess some things are universal.

A young man with a mass of unruly brown hair streaked blond at the tips was sitting draped across a swivel chair, displaying the dirty soles of his feet. "What we have is somebody most very clever. But not so clever as Liviu," he said.

The single narrow window, if Annja's sense of where they were in the Berlin tenement was correct, opened onto a narrow alley but was stifled with dark curtains. A little wan light from a cloudy late-afternoon Prussian sky filtered in at top and bottom. The rest of the illumination, such as it was, spilled from a thirty-inch LCD computer monitor that must have cost more than everything else in the tiny third-floor walk-up flat together, including the arcane gear, which had the look of salvage.

Behind the boy's narrow back, which was wrapped in a tatty dressing gown, Tex caught Annja's eye and winked. Evidently he did know where to find nerdage.

"Can you trace the IP address?" Tex asked.

"Not as such," Liviu said. His accent sounded as much Russian as Romanian to Annja, making her wonder where he'd learned to speak English. "It is phony as two-dollar bill, you know?"

Annja cocked a brow at Tex. He waggled his

eyebrows at her. "Forget it," he said. "He's on a roll."

"The path on your e-mail is also spoofed. Or rather, it is accurate, so far as it goes. It appears to originate from Universidad de Buenos Aires in Argentina. But it does not."

"No?" Annja asked.

Livia made a gesture of disgust. "Computer security in South America is legend for badness. Worse even than English corporate. Someone has broken in and made their system look as if it sent massage. But it is only relay."

Liviu turned to grin over his shoulder at Annja. "This tracing back is not so easy, you know. So is this important? Enough to pay important money?"

Tex laid a gentle hand on his shoulder. "We've been over this already, Liviu," he said in apparently friendly tones. "You're gettin' paid importantly enough. Don't you think?"

Annja saw the kid's shoulders tense. Apparently he read a threat she couldn't hear. Yet the adventure-show host's hand lay lightly on him.

"I need your help. Please. It's an emergency,"

she said in her, she hoped, passable Romanian. She spoke formally, not like an adult speaking to a child.

Liviu jumped as if stabbed. His two-tone hair flew out in all directions and then settled down in fresh random patterns around his head and face, making him look like a twenty-something Harry Potter who had gone horribly off the rails after graduating Hogwarts. His eyes were like the eyes of a tomcat that had just seen a twelve-foot-long monitor lizard waddle down its Berlin alley licking its scaly chops.

"You speak Romanian? You? America?"

"Yes. A little," she replied.

"Well," he said, "since I am a sucker for a pretty face, especially of so-famous Annja Creed, I will do it. Just for you, you understand?"

If I'm getting to be that famous it could start to be a problem, she thought.

Smiling, Tex started to pat the boy encouragingly on the shoulder.

Liviu batted him away, uttering a sharp statement.

Tex withdrew his paw. He looked hurt. "What'd he say?" he asked Annja.

"Don't touch me," she translated.

"Oh. Sorry."

"So," Liviu said, turning back to his keyboard with a flourish, "I penetrate UBA system, using the power of my mighty supercomputer, and—"

"Wait," Annja said. "Supercomputer?"

He nodded, making his hair flop back and forth like the crest of a chicken. "I have dozen Pentium I processors wired in massively parallel array. Makes supercomputer."

Annja raised a skeptical eyebrow at Tex, who shrugged.

"And so we see—"

"What?" Tex and Annja asked simultaneously.

"I fear there is no way to ascertain who has originated this e-mail. Even for Romanian boy genius with homemade supercomputer."

Tex's smile grew a little taut. "Son," he said, "if you're still thinking about jackin' us up for more money—" His tone stayed pleasant. But Annja noticed his accent got a lot more country.

But Liviu shook his head. "No, no. Would never dream. Truly I cannot find who. But I can find where."

He moved the mouse, clicked. A window appeared in the lower right-hand corner, showing a satellite shot from Google Earth.

"Northern Scotland?" Tex said.

Liviu typed rapidly. A circle appeared.

"Somewhere in here, your fake 419 e-mail comes from."

"The middle of the North Sea?" Annja said.

The boy shrugged. "So traffic analysis tells me. Is very clever software developed by your American NSA."

"You hacked into No Such Agency?" Tex exclaimed.

Liviu laughed. "Not even Liviu is so bold. I may be crazy but I am not insane. I do not wish to end like Karl of Chaos Computer Club, burned up in my Volkswagen in some woods."

"I thought the KGB did that," Tex said.

"So is said. But KGB, CIA, NSA—all same. You play in their games, one rule. You lose! No. National Security Agency generously shares its software with noble allies in the War on Terror. Not all are so very clever at trapping intruders. Is crippleware, no doubt. But it works enough, as you can see."

Annja felt her stomach start to sour. It's impossible! she thought. How will we ever find Jadzia now?

Tex started to clap the boy on the shoulder. His hand stopped an inch away, as if repelled by an invisible force field.

"Great job, Liviu," he said. "We'll take it from here."

Annja gave him a look of anguish. "Where?"

"Why, right where the man showed us, of course."

"But it's the middle of the North Sea!"

"Where we'll track it right on down." He showed her a big grin. "I told you. I know people."

"WHO IS ANNJA CREED?"

Jadzia had been roused from her cabin, which was small and spare and dank but not any less comfortable than anywhere else she'd been in this place. She was brought into an office with curling papers covering a metal desk and a desktop computer with noticeable monitor flicker. The bald bear of a man and his elegant compatriot were there with a couple of thugs.

She tossed her head and raised her chin defiantly. "How do you know our names?"

Before the big man could answer, Jadzia heard a commotion from the corridor outside. She wore the long shapeless sweater she had been given. Despite the perpetual chill of her unorthodox prison, her long pale legs were bare between the hem and her tennis shoes.

The man with white hair and lilac eyes set down the chipped ceramic bowl from which he had been eating steamed vegetables. His long double-breasted jacket was dark blue, with a stand-up collar that reminded Jadzia of Dr. Evil's suit in the Austin Powers movies.

"Your men, no doubt, Marshall," he said with distaste.

With a grunt and a grimace of irritation the larger man hefted himself to his feet from behind the desk littered with papers. He wore a red-checked flannel shirt and green work pants and reminded Jadzia, uncomfortably, of pictures of her father during his days as a Chicago plumber.

He went to the door of the little office.

"What?" he said, throwing open the faded green door. His name, Jadzia had learned, was Gus Marshall.

Three thugs in wool caps and bulky coats seemed to have charge of a bandy-legged little guy with a shaved head and dark beard, who wore a black T-shirt with a skull and crossbones and the legend, Kill 'Em All Let God Sort 'Em Out! over baggy forest-pattern camouflage pants.

"We caught Dobbs robbing stores from the pantry," said the biggest of the bunch, a Catalan with a slab face. "Again."

"You don't feed us enough!" the captive said in an unrepentant lower-class Manchester accent. "It's my bloody metabolism. I can't help it."

"Charles, Charles," Marshall said, shaking his head. For some reason the captive went pale and his face sagged, though the bigger man's tone was mild.

"We have rules," the elegant man said, his tone, as always, silky. His name was Sulin.

"It's not fair! You're supposed to bloody feed us decent! It's in the contract."

Marshall jerked his head sideways. The three hustled Dobbs into the office, which got very crowded. Jadzia backed up against a metal table with a derelict-looking coffee machine on it. Nobody was paying much attention to her. She entertained the thought of bolting for it but quickly kicked it to her mental curb. There was no place to go, even for a youthful genius who loved spy flicks.

"Your contract was quite explicit," Sulin said. "You get a fixed ration. We are totally dependent upon supplies brought by boat or helicopter, in case you have forgotten."

"When I signed I didn't know it was that small," Dobbs said sullenly. He seemed oppressed by the presence of Marshall, by something more than his sheer bulk, and sidled as though subconsciously toward Sulin.

"There have been budget cutbacks," Sulin said. "The recession—"

"Recession! But the price of bloody—"

"Enough," Marshall rumbled. He didn't raise his voice. He didn't have to. Just rolling around in that enormous chest before emerging gave his voice the sound of a volcano clearing its throat. "Hold out your hand."

"What?" Dobbs looked blank. Befuddlement momentarily overwhelmed his visible terror of the big man.

Marshall held out a hand that looked as if it had been carved from stone. "Your hand," he said. "Let me read your palm."

Sulin turned away with a sneer. "Superstitious nonsense," he muttered. It took him down a notch or two in Jadzia's esteem. Still, he was very pretty. In an abstract way she understood he was her captor, and certainly she looked forward to seeing him die. But that didn't really impinge on her consideration. She was a healthy young woman. She had needs. She idled with notions of seducing him, whereupon he'd fall in love with her—she being the heroine of her own personal film—and naturally help her escape.

Dobbs put his hand out toward Marshall as

eagerly as he would have thrust it into an open furnace. Marshall wrapped it in one of his. He looked like a father making sure his young son had washed up properly before dinner.

A bratwurst forefinger traced lines above the Englishman's palm. Marshall grunted.

"Lifeline's not too long, son," he said. "You should shape up. You aren't living right."

"So me mum always tells me," Dobbs said weakly.

"It also shows you're due for some misfortune in the very near future."

"Story of me life," Dobbs said. "Look, Mr. Marshall, I'm really sorry. I promise I'll never do it again. I'll pay the chopper boys to bring me in some nosh next trip."

"Yes, you will," Marshall said. The hand holding Dobbs's closed like a vise. With the other hand Marshall caught the little finger and broke it with a quick twist. It made a sound like a twig snapping.

Dobbs's scream made the crowded chamber ring like the inside of a giant bell.

"Take him to Pratkul and get that splinted," Marshall said. His voice sounded as if he were telling them what color paint to order to brighten up the place.

The three thugs jostled each other more than they did Dobbs as they dragged the sobbing man out of the office.

"Were you born in a barn?" Marshall called out. A hand came back in and pulled the door shut.

"Barbaric clown," Sulin said. "What do you think you're playing at?"

Lumbering back to his cracked black vinyl swivel chair behind the desk, Marshall shrugged. "Got to make an example every now and then. Fundamental management."

"Our principal pays for a Harvard MBA for you, and this is what you learn?"

"Pretty much. Granted, I got my own little ways of implementing the principles. But it's right in line with modern concepts."

Sulin shook his shock of hair. "How are we supposed to keep good help if you do that sort of thing?"

Marshall gave him a snaggle-toothed grin as he settled back into the chair. "I like ruling by fear," he said. "I guess you probably like to love 'em and turtle-dove 'em. Me, I find that if every once in a while I show them what happens to somebody who really annoys me, they find out their tolerance is pretty elastic."

He chuckled. "Anyway, the thought of trying to find another job that pays this well in this economy—that's real fear."

Sulin glared at him a moment longer. Then he sighed and turned his violet gaze to Jadzia. "Back to the subject of your friend, Ms. Creed," he said.

"How do you know our names, anyway?"

"Before she died, one of your pals at the dig talked to our people," Marshall said with evident relish. "They had to use a little *persuasion* on her. But don't worry. She didn't suffer long."

Jadzia glared blue laser death at him. "I hope to see you shot in the balls and falling to your death!" she snarled.

For a moment his gray boar-hog eyes got wide in amazement. Then he laughed. "That'd take a pretty unlikely set of circumstances, little girl. You'd better be ready to nurse a grudge through a bunch of reincarnations."

"Enough of this nonsense," Sulin said. "What do you know of Annja Creed?"

"I think she's some kind of special-force operator," Jadzia said. "Or maybe a cyborg."

One of the pair of Croats who had brought Jadzia to the room laughed. Sulin turned around and looked at the man. He said nothing. The man shut up.

"You might even be telling the truth," Sulin told Jadzia. "We have received some very curious reports from our agents who have had the misfortune to encounter her. It may be that yours is as good an explanation as anything else."

"What a load of baloney," Marshall said. "Those clowns are just making up stories because they don't want to admit they got whipped by a woman."

"Surely they realize the consequences of lying about a matter of such import," Sulin practically purred.

"And here your heart just bled all over me because I busted some limey slacker's pinkie finger," Marshall said.

Sulin shrugged. "We all must have standards, I suppose," he said. "And I suppose we agree that those standards must be enforced."

"Yeah. Otherwise, we got anarchy."

"And speaking of standards." Sulin turned to look at Jadzia. "You smell revolting. Have you not been permitted to use the showers? We have given explicit orders you are to be allowed privacy."

She scowled. He was being so stupid. It was very disenchanting. "Why should I bother with such trivial details?"

"Because other people got noses, sweetie," Marshall said.

"Go and clean yourself, or I shall scrub you myself," Sulin said.

She rallied to show him a big smile. "I might like that."

His violet eyes narrowed. "Then perhaps Marshall should scrub you instead."

Marshall guffawed. "That'd be fun," he said. "For me."

She spun on him. "You wouldn't—"

"Rape you? Naw. Not technically. But there

are plenty of things I could do that wouldn't leave a mark. At least, not that anybody could see."

Jadzia got very quiet. *This is real,* she thought. They might actually hurt me. The thought made her spirit shrivel.

"And remember," Marshall said, "we're on the clock, here. It's just ticking away. And once it runs out, all bets are off."

"Unless Annja Creed really is your friend, and seeks to help you," Sulin said. He smiled.

How did I ever think he was pretty? Jadzia wondered.

"In which case," he said, "we shall destroy her."

12

Annja and Tex were now Canadian citizens, complete with new passports and credit cards. Liviu had had some surprising equipment tucked into a closet of his crowded flat. She guessed that forgery had a lot more to do with the young Romanian's actual business model than systems invasion.

"Whose identities are we stealing?" Annja had asked after the boy snapped their pictures with a digital camera and went to work with a small scanner.

He laughed as if she had said something

absurd. He reminded her of Jadzia—half poignantly, half annoyingly.

"Nobody's," he said. "Welcome to virtual reality, complete with virtual people."

"But I thought it is supposed to be impossible to fake IDs."

"That shows what mundanes know," Liviu said, stabbing at his keyboard with two blindingly fast if slightly grubby fingers. "They really believe that shit. Making everything digital makes it so much easier. Nobody has to break in anywhere and change old high-school yearbooks now."

He studied the mug shot he had taken of Annja on his screen. After a quick glance she looked quickly elsewhere. The photo made her look bad enough to be official.

"But if it is in database, it must be true, yes? So now you are Alice Chapman and Matthew Wachowski of Toronto. You are schoolteacher and ministry of health investigator, respectively. You have lived together for three years. At end of questions remember to say, 'eh,' eh? Matthew has appendectomy scar from emergency surgery when he was seventeen."

"Hmm." Tex made a little quizzical noise. "I actually did have an emergency appendectomy. Real pain. Kind of an interesting coincidence that you—"

Liviu had turned his chair around and dropped his head to regard him from beneath arched brows.

"You're kidding," Tex said weakly.

"When you come to Liviu, you come to the best!"

They had spent the night in neighboring rooms at the ultraposh Westin Grand Berlin, under the Canadian identities Liviu had provided. Annja still felt vaguely guilty about who was being charged for their tickets and accommodations. Liviu had only laughed when she rather tentatively asked the question. She intuited it was some official agency he didn't like. That was probably most of them. Everywhere.

Tex had wakened her bright and early, looking eager, as if he had slept for fourteen hours, run ten miles and had himself a shower, a massage and a pot of coffee. She decided she hated him.

She reminded herself he was sparing no effort,

nor any of that rumored and now seemingly substantiated resourcefulness, to help a couple of strangers. And he seemed to be genuinely enjoying himself.

"You really were a cowboy?"

He shrugged. "Grew up on a ranch in Idaho. My parents both worked for the Forest Service. Ran cattle on the side. I was born in Massachusetts, though. They named me Mark. And I never set foot in Texas until I joined the Army and got sent to Fort Bliss."

The quickest route to their destination Tex had been able to work out on short notice entailed a plane trip from Templehof to Edinburgh and then a train ride to John o' Groat's on the extreme northern end of the island.

Annja chafed at every second it cost them. Jadzia was in deadly danger. She had received a second message from the kidnappers, likewise disguised as a 419 scam, this one supposedly from the daughter of dead Serbian strongman Slobodan Milošević, of all people. Its return path showed it "originated" from the California Department of Motor Vehicles. It gave an address for Annja to return an e-mail telling when and where she'd turn over the scrolls.

"Ask for more time," Tex had advised her. "It's pretty standard for negotiations like this." She had. Although neither one of them was a professional negotiator, she understood the mechanics of hostage taking—you kill your hostage, you're out of leverage.

Her face twisted before she could stop it. "Thinkin' about her?" Tex asked softly.

She nodded. Though she knew intellectually she had done the right thing, her guts knotted every time she did so. There were so many horrible things they could do to her, she knew.

"Don't."

She looked at nothing for a moment, then nodded.

"Where'd you get the nickname Tex?" she asked, making herself sound cheerful. She hoped it didn't sound as brittle to him as it did to her.

He winced. "In the Army. Most of my squaddies in basic were Easterners. To them anybody from west of the Mississippi was Texan. Especially someone who was indiscreet enough to admit he'd been a cowboy. I hate that name, but it's stuck like a bad debt."

"Why?"

"Because I hated it. The Army's like that. And of course the network publicists had to run with it."

Annja laughed. "You were really a Ranger?"

His expression didn't exactly harden. Maybe set a bit. After a moment, he sighed. "Yeah. It's public record. But don't go believing everything you hear about me. Especially around the network."

She pursed her lips. "Okay. Were you really an adventure outfitter in Alaska and Africa?"

"Yes."

"Survival instructor?"

"Uh-huh."

"Medical bush pilot in Central and South America?"

He sighed. "Yup."

"You've been busy."

"Ran away from home when I was fourteen. Worked in oil fields for a while, then as a hunting guide. Wasn't hard to pass for older—I've been this size since eighth grade."

"Were you abused as a child?" Annja asked with genuine concern.

He laughed. It was a rich laugh. It did not strike her as a laugh with much to hide. "Oh, heck no. The opposite, if anything. My parents were nice as they come. Maybe too nice. They converted to Buddhism when I was thirteen."

"Seriously?"

"Cross my heart. What really did it was the veganism." He shuddered theatrically. "If I never see another tofu, it'll be twenty years too soon."

"You ran away from veganism?"

"Can you think of a better reason? That, and the chores got boring. It was a real working ranch, cattle and horses, not some rich folks' fancy. Not sure how my folks rationalize raising beef cattle as vegetarians—they still do it, by the way. Being a cowboy ain't as romantic as the movies make out. So mainly I ran away to have adventures." He laughed. "Of all the reasons to run away, that's probably about the worst."

"But haven't you, well, *had* adventures?"

He looked at her with level blue eyes. "Yeah.

And that's the problem. *You've* had adventures, Annja. What'd they feel like?"

She thought for a moment. "Miserable. Mostly uncomfortable, inconvenient and scary."

"Me, too. Face it—adventure sucks."

She thought about that and found nothing to contradict. "Ever thought about quitting?"

"Oh, hell no. It's an addiction. I never tried crack, never even smoked cigarettes after my first one made me throw up. But I'm pretty sure the adventurous life hooks you worse. But what the hey—it's not like anyone gets out of this life alive, is it?"

His eyes danced. Annja laughed again. "No," she said. "I guess not."

JOHN O'GROATS WAS everything her heart could possibly have dreamed. Damp, gray, windswept and dismal. With sheep. Had the sun continued to shine, the land would have been dazzling green, between the boulders, anyway. But the sun refused to cooperate.

But outside was brilliant in comparison to the inside of the pub called the Jolly Wrecker. Es-

or an aging Gypsy aunt. She had a big nose and dark eyes in a well-upholstered olive face framed by long raven's-wing hair with dramatic silver streaks that flowed down her shoulders over the shawl with which she wrapped her generous form. Her dress seemed to have been made of myriad brightly colored scarves. The name was clearly ironic, Annja thought. She showed an abundance of bustling motherly energy and cheer.

"Phil," Suze said with a tut-tut for punctuation, "the e-mail said they would. And anyway, dear Tex is family."

"It's always good to hear," Phil said with an expansive gesture. "Always make things explicit, say I."

"That's the law of good old B6," rasped the an who loomed over his right shoulder like a eleton at a feast.

"The sequel to *Babylon 5?*" Annja asked, ildered. She had gone into TV-trivia mode, ng at last recognized *The Prisoner* as the s cult show starring Patrick McGoohan.

ack Bart's Bloody Buggerin' Broadcastin'

pecially the back room, with the sweating ancient wooden barrels and dust-coated bottles stacked around the sod walls. Despite the fact it was half-dug into a hillock, the wind whistled in the rafters and occasionally down the back of Annja's neck where she sat in a chair that seemed to possess no two legs of equal length. The pub had grass on the roof and a weathered sign with the image of a jolly-looking sport with a peg leg and a grappling anchor, dressed in a yellow rain slicker and what she would have called a sou'wester. She suspected the place had started life as a shepherd's hut.

Some places reeked of quaintness, others of atmosphere. The Jolly Wrecker mostly reeked of lanolin, although stale alcohol, mildew and faint but persistent hints of decay played their little parts. Even with the dim bare bulb, which must have pulled all of five watts, hanging far enough from the already low wood-beamed ceiling on its frayed cord to threaten Annja's cranium, it was like being inside a ship's hold.

"So," said the fat man with the greasy gray-and-brown locks spilling down around the shoulders of the dark blue rainslicker he wore over a dark pullover, "what can we do you for?"

Stop with the lame eighties one-liners, Annja had to forcibly restrain herself from answering.

Tex leaned forward and rested a forearm on the moist round table. Although his chair was as functionally unstable as hers, she noticed it didn't rock. Whereas every time she breathed one of her chair legs thumped accusingly on the warped plank floor.

"Information," Tex said, smiling. "We want information."

"You won't get it," the man across from him said promptly.

Tex's eyebrows shot up. Annja almost felt relief at seeing him nonplussed for once.

"It's a quote from *The Prisoner*," said the woman who sat beside the fat man. "An old series on the telly." She reached over to pat a pudgy hand almost as burdensomely beringed as her own. "Be a dear, Phil, and show our guests a little consideration. They've had a long journey."

"Sorry, luv. Can't help me'self. I can resist anything but temptation, you know."

"That and bad jokes," the woman replied.

The man looked back to Tex with dark eyes that danced despite the gloom. He had a keg head on a barrel body, a beard and a mustache with turned-up tips and in general a strong resemblance to dead British actor Oliver Reed, who had always been a favorite of Annja's, clandestinely watching movies in the TV room after the sisters had gone to bed. He calle[d] himself Phil Dirt. He looked like an old m[an] passed through a life of extreme ups [and] downs and going at last to seed, albe[it] without a fight.

"Magic words?" he said.

"Huh?" Tex said. He blinked. He [felt] adrift at the stout man's earlier resp[onse,] abrupt but not unfriendly question [pushed him] further out to sea. "Please?"

"We'll pay," Annja said hastily[.]

Phil brightened visibly. "The [   ]

The woman who sat beside[   ] head without looking up from [   ] had been introduced as Vici[   ] looked like was a youngish[   ]

Brood," said what appeared to be a vaguely conical mass of abandoned brush standing by the barrels over Phil Dirt's left shoulder. Surreptitiously Annja counted the *B*s on her fingers. Closer inspection through the gloom, conducted earlier when the leader of the crew had introduced the man by the unlikely moniker of Ob Noxious, showed him to be an enormous fat guy with a nose like a large-pored potato and two murky green eyes squinting out from more graying blond hair and beard than seemed humanly possible. He looked to Annja as if, should you toss a bucket or two of green paint over him, he could play the Swamp Thing in a movie without recourse to special effects. Or even makeup.

"So you call yourselves Black Bart's Bloody Buggerin' Broadcastin' Brood," Annja repeated, trying desperately to understand why Tex had brought her here.

"Right," said the man to Phil's right. "One of the last free-range pirate radio crews in the British Isles, we are." He was called Lightnin' Rod, and seemed to be the station's power-plant guy. He was tall and cadaverous, with long lank black hair just touched with gray, a long, droopy black handlebar mustache and black eyes.

Annja sneaked a sidewise glance at Tex. She didn't believe in ESP, but all the same she beamed a thought at him: I hope you know what you're doing.

He winked at her.

"Since the music-hall routine will never end, otherwise," Vicious Suze said, her plump fingers moving like hummingbirds around a butterfly bush at her knitting, "what sort of information did you have in mind, ducks?"

"Anomalous traffic in the sea north of here," Tex said.

"Surface? Air? Radio?" Phil Dirt asked.

"Yes."

He raised an eyebrow at the American, then chuckled. "Aye."

"Boats, helicopters," Rod said. "See 'em all the time, buzzing off to sea."

"Do you know where they go?" she asked.

Phil looked at her a moment with an appreciative twinkle in his eye. With something like a shock she realized he was ogling her. She didn't know whether to be horrified or flattered.

He sighed. "No idea, I'm afraid."

"Can you find out?" Tex asked.

"Gannet can," Rod rasped.

"Who's Gannet?"

"Gannet Hundredmind," Phil said. A corner of his mustache quirked up in evident amusement as he said it. Another in-joke, Annja figured. She refused to ask.

"Our boy wonder in residence," said Vicious Suze, knitting away. "He's all that keeps us on the air, you know."

"Can you take us to him?" Annja asked.

Phil Dirt smiled hugely. "Just how adventurous are you feeling, luv?"

"What makes me think," she said, "there's no right answer to that question?"

13

"Adventures," Annja muttered to Tex as the black Zodiac boat bottomed between two-story North Sea waves. The seat slammed her tailbone again. A spray of saltwater drenched her anew. Her hair felt as if she had soaked it with an entire bottle of some toxic hairspray, from all the salt. "Why does it always have to be adventures?"

Her companion had his head up and his jaw set in a somewhat fixed smile. "What'd I tell you earlier?"

In the stern, Lightnin' Rod steered, looking even more pirate-like with a black head rag sporting a skull and crossed cutlasses tied over his lengthy windblown locks. Having seen the same logo on a T-shirt sporting the legend Pirates of the Internet, worn by a geek from the tech department of the television station, Annja knew the kerchief probably came from some online store. She wasn't sure whether that added or detracted from the effect.

Ahead of them the Gannet C drilling platform rose slowly out of the gloom like a giant battle robot from some science fiction yarn. A few lights shone yellow and furtive from its bulk in the overcast early evening. Abandoned in the early nineties by British Petroleum after it ran too dry to remain economical to operate, the platform had become the haven and broadcasting station for Black Bart's bunch. The John o' Groat's contingent were cramped into the black inflatable power craft looking as serene as if bashing through sea were no more strenuous than a stroll in Hyde Park.

In among the shadowed pillars that formed the legs of the station, they found a welded metal ladder awaiting them. With a theatrical gesture Phil Dirt waved them to go up first. Tex in turn deferred to Annja.

Annja put a hand on a rung. It was cold and slick. Just the way she expected. Oh, well, she thought, no one is shooting at me.

She climbed. Tex followed.

"Our friends are being pretty magnanimous letting us go first," he called when they were twenty or so feet up.

"I just kind of figured Phil did it so he could watch my butt," Annja said.

"Well, that's certainly among the fringe benefits, ma'am. But, going first, if we slip and fall we fall on them. As opposed to vice versa."

"I feel so special."

"RIGHT," the young man said, rubbing together hands in fingerless gloves. "Let's see what we have, then."

The main engineering room at the heart of Black Bart's broadcasting station was a boxy steel womb lined with racks and racks of equipment of unknown purpose. The various tiny multi-colored blinking lights and indicators provided all the illumination except for a few amber blackout foot lamps. It added to the sense of claustrophobia, as well as giving Annja the impression of being surrounded by hundreds of psychedelic rats.

Gannet Hundredmind swiveled on his stool, flipping switches to the left and right, at seeming random. Annja and Tex stood behind him. Annja tried hard not to hover. Tex looked centered and relaxed and in general as if he was having a fine old time. But then, he always looked like that.

Lightnin' Rod had stayed with the Zodiac boat when the others went up, apparently to berth it somewhere. Making her apologies, the matronly Suze had vanished after the climb to the platform, a chilly collection of rusty pipes and metal bulkheads, saying she wanted to tend to dinner. The others who had met the Americans in the Jolly Wrecker escorted them through a warren of dimly lit passages that echoed to the sounds of their footsteps, with water incessantly dripping from overhead. Now they stood in a clump at the back of the control center and chatted while young Gannet worked his magic.

"Sodding podcasts," Phil was saying to a stocky guy with a fluorescent pink Mohawk, jug-handle ears and a pug's face, who wore grimy dark coveralls. He was Stan the Man McLeod, the physical plant engineer who kept the place as livable as it was—which, on first impression, wasn't very, although Annja suspected he deserved huge credit for keeping it habitable at all in the chill and hostile environment. He poured a sable ferret named Isadora from one big, stained, scarred, crack-nailed fist to the other without seeming to notice. "They're stealing our audiences right out from beneath our noses, they are."

"It's a terrible thing," added Rod, who had just slid in the door. "The pigs couldn't shut us down for decades of tryin' their black-hearted best. And here we are getting done down by Silicon bleeding Valley!"

"We get all manner of chatter on the air up here," Gannet said. The young broadcast engineer had turned back to his monitor. He wore grimy cargo pants and several layers of sweaters over what was evidently a skinny young frame, so that his head stuck on a thin neck out of an incongruously huge mass of clothing. He looked like a plush toy turtle. "Satellite phone broadcasts, other radio traffic. It's increased a great deal the past few months. Never paid much mind to it before this, though."

"Can you listen in on any of the traffic?" Annja asked.

Gannet gave her a questioning look. He had pale skin that in the glow looked blue-white, and moist, almost purplish lips. "Oi, that would be unethical, now, wouldn't it?" he commented in a lilting Liverpudlian accent. Then he grinned. "Not that that slowed me down much. But the phone traffic is all encrypted. The rest is bloody banal. Talking to ships, the odd helicopter, that sort of thing. If I had to guess, I'd say somebody else has occupied another old rig like this rattletrap. Only they're a bit better funded than we are."

"Kids these day," Rod was saying, shaking his gaunt-cheeked head. "They've no appreciation for the fact we do this out of love. Not like when we was young."

"Do you know which platform?" Annja asked.

Gannet shook his shaggy head. "There's a dozen it could be. More. Sorry."

"Can you triangulate the traffic?" Tex asked.

The boy held up a forefinger. "Ah," he said. "That we can do."

His fingers danced over his keyboard.

"Gotcher!" Gannet crowed, calling his elders from the back of the room. A map appeared, showing an angular mass of land narrowing into the northeast, breaking into a trickle of islands, as if squeezed from a cake froster with a tendency to drip. A red cross showed in the water above and to the left of the last island.

"We've our latitude and longitude. Now let's see what's there."

The map shrank and moved to the left of the screen. A text box appeared, and next to it the image of what appeared to be a Cubist mountain rising from the sea. The box showed the bolded words, Claidheamh Mór B.

"Cl—cl—whoa," Tex said. He looked at Annja, who shook her head.

"Sorry. I don't do Gaelic."

"Ah, but you should," said Gannet. "Just say it Claymore B, and you'll not be far off. That's what it means." He clicked some more at his keys. "Abandoned 1998. Bought in 2002 by a then newly formed oil consortium called Euro Petro."

"I've heard of them," Annja said. "I've seen their commercials."

Tex nodded. "I don't know about you," he said, "but something about that perky self-righteousness about how environmentally and socially conscious they are just goes right down my spine like a cheese grater."

"Me, too."

"Especially since it's all a sham," Gannet said cheerfully. "They deserve the name pirates far more than our lot."

"What do you mean?" Annja asked. "I thought the European Union was the majority owner."

"And that makes a difference how?" Gannet asked. "Most of the world's known oil reserves are owned by government companies. All just a matter of what you call the thieves in charge, innit?"

Phil Dirt came up and laid a meaty ring-laden hand on his shoulder. "Noble work, boy," he said in his deep voice. "But you've got to do something about that uncontrollable cynicism about government. That's not what anarchy's all about."

"THAT'S AN AIRPLANE?" Annja asked.

"Sure is," Tex said with satisfaction. He was holding his Stetson on his head against the brisk salt wind with one hand. "An ultralight. Hand-built with love. And no small measure of genius."

"Uh-huh," she said, shading her eyes against the morning glare. "Just one question."

"What's that?"

"Where do you put the key to wind it up?"

The aircraft—Annja had a hard time thinking of it as an *airplane*—whined past them down the narrow strip. It didn't look much like an airplane. It had a big pod-shaped cockpit enclosed in wraparound glass, a single fuselage and a high wing. But where it parted company with real airplanes, to Annja's mind, apart from being the size of a Volkswagen Beetle, was that it kept its propeller at the rear of its high-mounted wing. That, she thought, was just wrong.

She could see it well deserved its moniker of

ultralight, and suspected that was why, after a very short landing run, it slowed and turned to taxi back toward them at the pace of a brisk walk. Annja noted the landing strip was very short indeed. For all its picturesque desolateness and quaint sense of ends-of-the-earth isolation, on the northerly Orkney Island of Papa Westray there wasn't room for anything else.

"How you feelin'?" Tex asked.

"I feel as if I'm filled with ants," she told him, "and an earthquake just hit the mound."

He nodded. "I hear you. We got plenty to do," he said. "It'll take your mind off worrying."

"Did I ever tell you how much I hate positive thinking?" Annja said. He only laughed at her.

The little craft came whining up to them. Annja tried hard not to think about mosquitoes. It stopped as a young woman in coveralls and a ball cap came dashing out from the airfield shack to stick fat wooden wedges under its tricycle landing gear. A door opened beneath the wing and a short man with short white hair, a snowy mustache and aviator shades popped out.

"Tex!" he exclaimed. He strutted forward, sticking out his hand.

"Leo!" Tex shook, and then they embraced briefly. Either the little English aviator was accustomed to such typically American intimacy or he faked it well.

He turned to the young woman. "Thank you much, my dear," he said. She nodded, grinned and scampered back inside.

"Annja," Tex said, "I'd like you to meet my old buddy, Leo." He smiled and spoke with great enthusiasm, as if reunited with his very best friend after decades. From spending a couple of days in his company Annja guessed he'd display the same enthusiasm if he was meeting a stranger for the first time. And it would be, so far as she could tell, entirely genuine, each and every time. "Leo, Annja Creed."

"A pleasure," she said, shaking his dry hand. It felt as if he could crack walnuts with it, although his touch was no more than a firm, quick squeeze.

"My pleasure, Ms. Creed."

He turned away with a look close to genuine

alarm on his face. "My soul, who are these people? Did a caravan of travelers somehow make their way out here to Papa Westray?"

"These people" were Phil Dirt, Vicious Suze, Lightnin' Rod and Ob Noxious. "Travelers," Annja knew, was what the British called Gypsies. The motley bunch were trotting out from the little cluster of low structures beside the airfield toting bulging knapsacks and rolls of blue groundsheets. Despite the punk names, they were dressed more in the fashion of long-leftover hippies. Annja surmised that punk had in the end just been a phase for them. Their rest state was perpetually the Summer of Love.

"So you're the intrepid aviator," Phil Dirt boomed in his best Shakespearean baritone, rolling forward with hand extended.

Leo shook his hand with good if bewildered grace. "I say," he said, "what *are* your people doing?"

"Let's go inside," Tex said, taking the pilot by the shoulder and tugging him gently toward the buildings. "Leo designed and built this aircraft himself, Annja. He's a wizard that way. Total legend in the aviation world. Test-flew England's first supersonic bomber in the early sixties. Even did a stint at Edwards."

"But my *Ariel*—" Leo said.

Rod and Ob were unrolling the shiny blue tarps around the aircraft and weighting them down with head-sized chunks of rock. Kneeling, Suze was unpacking big rolls of masking tape and cans of spray paint. Phil's job seemed to be to shake the cans to make sure they rattled properly.

"She'll be fine, Leo, just fine. The paint'll wash right off. And if it doesn't, my show will pay for a nice new paint job. The old girl could use a fresh coat, couldn't she?"

As he towed the little Englishman away he winked at Annja over his shoulder. Annja wondered exactly what it indicated. Either that he was actually footing the bill himself, she guessed, or that he already had a plan in mind to get some kind of *Past Master* episode out of this escapade. He had displayed himself abundantly ready to bend or even break regulations and laws in what he thought was a good cause.

"I've used her on the show a few times," Tex said to Annja. "*Ariel* and I go way back."

"There isn't any risk to her, is there, Tex?" Leo asked plaintively.

"I'll take as good care of her as I do my own precious hide," Tex said. "I'm not a stuntman, after all, Leo. You know that. I don't get paid to take foolish risks. Now, come on. There's a fresh-brewed pot of coffee waiting for you inside. Oh, and if memory serves, a bottle of thirty-year-old single malt with your name on it."

"CLAIDHEAMH MÓR B is a pretty standard fixed offshore drilling platform, as you can see here, kiddies," Gannet said, pointing to the screen of a notebook computer that was so wide Annja could hardly think of it as portable. It gave a big, beautiful picture of the platform from above, Annja had to admit.

The radio nerd had ridden the Zodiac with them over twenty miles or so of North Sea to the northernmost island of the Orkney group from Gannet C, where Annja and Tex had spent the night on air mattresses in adjoining dank metal cells.

"Here's a night shot," Gannet said. The image twinkled with points of light.

"It's pretty," Annja said abstractedly. She was having trouble focusing, even though this briefing was vital.

The extension Jadzia's captors had conceded, in their cleverly coded e-mails, was due to run out at sunset. The plan called for Annja and Tex to infiltrate Claidheamh Mór B in the dark. And the real-time satellite weather image, currently resident in a small but readily discernible window in the lower left-hand corner of Gannet's screen, showed a nasty roiling mass of storm—a typical North Sea blow. Despite the clarity of the day, the storm was due to hit the platform about the same time they were.

It was a good thing the diminutive pilot was in the airfield office in an adjoining building, getting expansive on venerable whiskey with the aging airplane buffs who ran the strip, Annja thought. Indeed, a small crowd had gathered, moving somewhat slowly and smelling of wool. Pretty much the island's entire collection of aviation fans had gotten wind of the unusual craft's arrival and turned up to look on in awe and be regaled.

"And here's another overhead from daytime," Gannet said. "Notice here on the southwest corner of the platform."

Annja squinted. A little white tadpole shape was visible in the middle of a big yellow circle. It hadn't been visible in the previous images.

"That's from this morning," Gannet said.

"Shit," Tex said. "Pardon my French."

"That would be 'merde,' Tex," Annja said.

"I knew that."

As Gannet zoomed in on the image the tadpole grew into an unmistakable helicopter. "That looks just like the helicopter that we—saw in Italy," Annja exclaimed. She stopped herself just short of blurting "attacked." They had not told the Black Bart crew any details of just what they were doing, and they had not pressed. For all the air of make-believe about the radio pirates, they really were outlaws of a sort. They knew the value of discretion.

The coverall-clad airfield girl stuck her head in the door. Without the ball cap, she had blond hair tied in pigtails and a wide face full of freckles. She didn't really look like Jadzia, but her appearance still gave Annja a brief twinge.

"Your golf gear's here, Mr. Tex!" she chirped.

"Thanks a bundle, Maggie," Tex said.

"Golf gear?" Annja said, a beat out of sync with Gannet.

Tex shrugged. "Hey, you never know when I might fancy a round, as you Brits would say. Addiction's like that."

The youth gave him a dubious look. He transferred it to Annja, who shrugged.

"I doubt it's the same chopper you saw in Italy," Tex said. "Be a long, slow trip."

Gannet clicked again. The chopper grew to fill the screen. Annja studied it.

"I'm pretty sure it's the same model, though," she said. "Same paint scheme, too. Blue with white trim."

"Which might mean it belongs to the same people." Tex shrugged. "Or it may not. Pretty common color scheme."

"AgustaWestland A109," said Gannet. "Fairly common design, that. But what we can do is read the registration number off the tail boom." He typed some more. "And here we see the machine is registered to EP Great Britain, operating out of their Edinburgh facility."

"Which pretty much confirms what we know already, doesn't it?" Annja asked.

"Suggests EP still owns the rig, anyway," Tex said.

She frowned. "What would an oil company want with a tapped-out drilling platform?"

"Well," Gannet said, sitting back and lacing his fingers behind his head, "I can't speak for them, but we find ours right handy for illicit activities."

"STORM'S COMING in fast," Annja said from the doorway. "Poor Jadzia." The two sentences weren't exactly related. Poor Jadzia was based on the imminent expiration of the kidnappers' deadline. Then again, it was looking more and more likely the storm would hit Claidheamh Mór B before they did. Each second it delayed them made the captive girl's survival less likely. And if the terrible North Sea swallowed them in its fury…

The multiple metallic clack from behind her in the airfield's little maintenance shop made the hairs on Annja's nape rise. Not because it was unfamiliar, or for that matter that she was afraid of it. She knew perfectly well what made a sound like that. Nothing else on Earth did. The unexpectedness of hearing it *here* was what shocked her.

"You know how to use one of these?" Tex sat on a plastic crate with his hat pushed way back on his head. He was holding up a black shotgun with a rear pistol grip. "Benelli M4 semiauto combat shotgun, 12-gauge. The very latest thing in social work—auto regulating, gas operated, with two stainless-steel self-cleaning pistons. The Marines use 'em, but they're good weapons in spite of that."

"I've used a shotgun a few times, yes," Annja said guardedly. "Never a Benelli before."

"Nothing to it. Loads here. Ghost-ring sight, just the thing for rapid target acquisition." He cycled the charging handle. "Point and shoot. I'd recommend something a little lighter on the recoil—truth to tell, 12-gauge is a bit much for most men to use efficiently. But all your work with that sword of yours gives you a little bit of an edge when it comes to strength, don't you think?"

He looked up and saw her expression. "What?"

Annja glanced around. Tex had cheerfully chased everyone out of the shop before opening up his long, heavy "golf bags." Leo had headed back to the mainland by motorboat-taxi to spend the night. Gannet and crew were out admiring their handiwork repainting the ultralight.

"One question," she said. "Aren't the Orkney Islands still part of the United Kingdom?"

"Last I checked," Tex said, laying the shotgun on a bench beside him and fishing out a pair of black autopistols.

"Don't they have gun control here?"

"Sure do. Along with a skyrocketing rate of violent home invasions. No connection, I'm sure. Why?"

She looked at him.

"Oh. These?" He laughed and laid them down on a cloth spread on the tabletop, being careful, she observed, not to point them at her.

"As for these, well—they're legal. As to how legal it is for us to have them—" he shrugged "—don't ask, don't tell, as the saying goes."

He grinned at her persistently dubious look. "I told you I had contacts."

She laughed a bit feebly. "Whatever you say." It occurred to her she didn't really need to know the whole truth. And, thinking about it, she didn't really want to.

He tossed her a cardboard box of fifty 9 mm cartridges and poured a cloth bag of empty black magazines onto the table. "We've got an hour or so before our flight leaves for Claymore B. Hope your thumb's up for a workout."

14

"Dang," Tex said. He didn't say it loud. Annja was surprised she could hear it over the reverberations of that last thunder crack. Her ears literally rang.

"What? What 'dang'? 'Dang' does not sound good."

"Depends on your definition of 'not good.'"

"Try me."

"Just lost GPS."

"The lightning bolt did that? I didn't know lightning could knock it out."

He shrugged despite the sheer physical effort of keeping the little airplane under control in the brutal winds. Annja suddenly realized just how difficult that must have been with no power assist on a plane that size. "Might just be the storm blocks the signal. One way or another we're flying by dead reckoning now."

"It never occurred to me until now," Annja said, "just how ominous that phrase is. Can you really find the platform without it?"

The rig, which had seemed so huge and intimidating when she and Tex had worked out their tactics for infiltrating it, shrank in her mind to the dimensions of a Matchbox model in this vast and hateful sea.

"Well," Tex said, drawing it way out, "I can give it the old college try."

"What if we miss it in the storm? This rain is like lead curtains at times."

"Lemme put it this way—got a hankerin' to see the Arctic up close and personal?"

"We can make it all the way to the ice pack?"

"Oh, shoot, no. I'm just funnin' you, ma'am. We'll run out of fuel and ditch in the sea long before that. The good news is, it's a short-enough hop from Papa Westray to the platform. We don't see it in the next five minutes, we've got plenty of leeway to double back and try a quartering search."

"What if we still can't find it?"

"Then we'll be well and truly lost. As opposed to just lost."

"I love a man who knows how to show a girl a good time."

"We aim to please, ma'am."

THE BIG MAN SAT in a chair, oblivious to the spray the wind lashed against the window of the commissary. A generator-run space heater blasted away, turning a far corner of the room into a localized furnace. He was out of its baleful radiance, but cushioned by layers of clothing, fat and a genuine indifference to his own comfort, he ignored the chill that inevitably seeped in from the storm outside.

Sulin stood by the window, as far as possible from his coleader, with his hands clasped behind the back of his high-collared jacket, gazing out into the storm.

For some reason, both turned and looked at Jadzia. The girl sat eating a bar of jerky, tearing at the tough strip with sharp white teeth. She had been semicovertly admiring Sulin. She almost regretted that Annja Creed would inevitably kill him.

Something in her manner seemed to irk Marshall. "Time is running out for you, girl," he rumbled.

Sulin stiffened slightly. "It's true that the ultimatum has expired," he said. "But we are to wait for further orders from above before we take any action, my friend."

"I'm not your friend, pretty boy," Marshall said without looking at him. His small gray eyes gazed intently at Jadzia, who ostentatiously crossed her long bare legs.

"Your little gal pal must not really care about you," he told her. "She's gone to ground to protect her own precious hide. But we'll find her and dig her out. And we'll get the scrolls."

"Don't hector her," Sulin said. "It's doubtful she knows anything of real use, to us or our superiors."

"What about what they've read from the scrolls so far?"

"Presumably all the truly sensational revelations they have come across are contained in what they posted on the Net," Sulin said. "If they found more, it died with the rest of the dig team."

He glanced over his shoulder at Marshall. A flash of lightning lit his beautifully sculpted face in harsh purple-white radiance. "Beware of asking questions that might have dangerous answers," he said with contempt ringing through his voice. "If she did happen to know something more, something…controversial—would it be healthy for you or for me to hear it? This whole operation is about keeping these things secret."

"You threatening me?" Marshall laughed.

Sulin's violet eyes narrowed. "Do not delude yourself," he said in a voice of oiled silk. "We are tools, purchased by our employers. Will they think twice about discarding us if they deem our usefulness has come to an end?"

Marshall stretched and sighed. "Shit, Lucy," he said. "You figure anybody leaves this world alive?"

"Louis," Sulin hissed.

Jadzia rose. Her mood had shifted. She didn't take Marshall's menace particularly seriously.

He was a sadistic thing, certainly. But Jadzia was the star of this adventure.

She was the heroine of this saga, she decided. And the heroine never dies.

Without a word she walked from the room.

GLANCING OUT the port side of the wraparound canopy, Annja saw a great gray monster of a wave crest above the level of their tiny aircraft. She understood intellectually the need to fly so low—so that the ocean's surface effect would hide them from the radar rig Gannet's satellite imaging had clearly shown rotating high up in Claidheamh Mór B's superstructure.

But the sight of those menacing waves filled her with terror. The North Sea was not known for its mercies.

It took all her will to control the fear. But she did. She held on to *self*. To focus.

She formed a picture in her mind—a young, pretty face, framed by blond pigtails. Jadzia. The innocent whose destiny she had cradled in her own two hands. And dropped. She would not let herself fail Jadzia again. If she died trying—well, she would die trying her very damned best.

To distract herself from the crashing menace of the storm, she let loose a question that had been bubbling around in her subconscious for days.

"Why are you helping me, Tex?"

"Huh?" he shouted back over his shoulder. She saw his face ran with sweat, although it was cool in the aircraft despite the efforts of its tiny heater. His shoulders hunched and bunched with effort, he grunted with the strain of fighting the yoke. His brow was folded with concentration, yet his eyes and mouth smiled as if he were having the time of his life.

"Why are you helping me?"

He actually paused. In their brief acquaintance she had seldom seen him do that. He was thoughtful, analytical even, during the downtimes, as she had seen again that afternoon planning their quixotic two-person aerial assault on the oil platform. But in the crunch, when called upon he never seemed to hesitate to speak or act as the situation demanded.

"I can't resist a pretty face?" he called back at length.

Fury surged up inside her. "Don't try to blow me off! Not now. This is important."

At once she felt remorseful, and also stupid. He is risking terrible danger for you and Jadzia, she thought. But Tex answered with regret audible in his words, if scarcely above the booming of the wind and the constant cannonade of thunder near and far.

"You're right," he said, shouting to be heard with his face turned forward again toward their unseen goal. "You deserve a straight answer. When I was a kid I did some things. They may or may not have been illegal. You might say I had official status to do them, in fact. I told myself they couldn't be wrong if duly constituted authority told me to do them. And that they were for the greater good, you know?"

He shook his head. "Later on I found what we'd been told was mostly lies. I watched my buddies die, for lies. And you know, my real reason for it all was that I was a stupid, self-centered kid who thought he'd live forever no matter what. And doing what they told me to gave a dirty, dangerous thrill like nothing else."

"That's why you're doing this? For the thrill?" Again she regretted that the unbearable seethe of emotion inside her, no less tempestuous than the sky and sea outside, had propelled the first thought to pop in her mind straight out her mouth.

"Maybe," he yelled back. "I been chasin' thrills ever since, even though they're all pretty feeble imitations of—of what I used to do. But I feel I've got something to make up for. And I'm grateful for a chance to do something real— something I know is good. Shoot, Annja. It's a *little girl* out there."

Her right arm shot forward past his shoulder. "Look!" she cried.

A single light glowed in the darkness like a white eye. It was just a few points away from dead ahead.

"Now comes the fun part," Tex said, all business again. He climbed a few scant yards to give them clearance from the thousand avid mouths of the sea, for the plane would lose lift in a turn.

He flew level a moment longer, to regain speed. Then he banked the ultralight left.

Out into the open sea.

JADZIA STALKED down a corridor with greenish enamel coming away from the metal in flakes, leaving splotches of fungus in muted psyche-delic colors on the bulkhead. Her assurance of moments before had evaporated. Maybe it was the creepy surroundings, and the horrible cease-less moaning of the sea, the creaking of the rig, the cannonading of the rising storm.

None of the noises was as terrible as the voice in her head that kept trying to tell her, They're right. She's not coming. You're all alone.

Of course, she'd *always* been all alone. Alone in a world of stupid people.

Captive though she was, Jadzia was allowed total freedom to roam the platform. It wasn't as if she could escape. There were boats, surely. But she wasn't about to head out at random into the middle of the ocean. Even her fantasy adven-ture thoughts had their limitations. Nor was she under any illusion she could fly the sleek helicopter tied invitingly to the southwest corner of the platform.

No, Annja was coming for her. Jadzia was sure of that. She had no other option.

On a whim she decided to drop in on the security room. Even creepy company was better than being alone with her fears. It was a level down from the commissary, down a ringing, rattling metal stair.

Inside were banks of monitors showing visual feeds from cameras positioned all about the rig, and a pair of Albanians ostensibly watching them. A Walther machine pistol lay ostentatiously across a table near one of them.

They looked up and emitted guarded hellos. The younger one smiled; the older man frowned. Like all of the more than twenty personnel Jadzia had encountered on the steel island, they spoke English as the common tongue, and their native language when they fell in with countrymen. They took for granted they were talking secret code that no one else could understand.

That was the reason she decided to stop there. She found Albanian fascinating, though ugly.

Though Indo-European, it had no living languages as relatives. It therefore tied in with her love of ancient languages, as well as the weird in general. Plus it gave her something to do.

Apparently the men felt flattered by her presence.

"She fancies me," the younger man said.

"Imbecile," the older man replied. He spoke without heat. He had an air of having been there and having done that. Jadzia's grasp of the niceties wasn't up to telling her whether it was a pose or not.

"Why does she keep sniffing around us, then?"

"Who knows? Perhaps she is a demon, sniffing for your soul."

"Hah," the young man said. But he looked at Jadzia warily.

"What bothers me most," the older man said, "is that while she's here we cannot drink." The monitors were flashing images from around the rig, but the man paid no attention. Clearly, there was nothing interesting to see out on the raging sea.

Jadzia propped her rump against the edge of a table and let her eyes drift lazily over the other monitors.

Then they backtracked quickly. And went wide.

15

A squall broke like a dark sheet ripping apart before their eyes. Through the rain-streaked windscreen Annja abruptly saw it. A rectilinear steel castle, its pylons obscured by waves and mist and blowing sheets of rain, seemed to float in the air before them.

It had been a masterful feat of flying by Tex, swinging deliberately wide of the station in order to approach from out to sea, the direction from which traffic was least likely to come, hence least likely to be closely watched. But relief was crowded from Annja's mind by a new throng of fears. The platform looked awfully close.

"Doesn't it take runway space even for *Ariel* to taxi to a stop?" Annja asked.

"Usually," Tex said.

"And aren't we, well, kind of *low?*"

"I'm bagging two birds with one cliché," he said.

He had already throttled the engine suspiciously low. The ultralight wallowed in the heavy turbulent air mere feet above the waves like a moth over a flame. Suddenly he pulled the yoke into his flat stomach. *Ariel*'s nose came up. She soared.

The grim gray cliff of steel seemed close enough to touch. Annja braced for impact.

Her muscles taut as piano wires, Annja watched the dark, tangled underside of the platform rushing by outside. Then suddenly they passed the upper edge of the deck. At the same time she felt the airplane lose lift as gravity sucked away its momentum. The nose dropped as a last surge of forward movement carried the craft about ten feet inboard, where it fell on its landing gear with a tailbone-jarring thump and stopped dead.

As JADZIA WATCHED, amazed, a tiny airplane, oddly shaped and bizarrely painted in drab squiggly streaks, popped into view like a dolphin jumping from its tank at an aquatic show. It slammed down hard on the steel deck of the drilling platform.

The Albanians were talking animatedly about what bastards Sulin and Marshall were, using plenty of hand gestures. They hadn't seen the aircraft appear on the screen behind them.

Jadzia pushed off from the table, made herself walk deliberately, angling to place her skinny body between the monitor and the guards. A lean man she had never seen before popped out of the tiny craft. A moment later the unmistakable form of Annja Creed scrambled out into rain that surrounded her with a waist-high mist of impact-exploded raindrops.

Jadzia's steps wobbled slightly as the sinews holding her knees together seemed to turn to rubber bands. She reached a hand up to the monitor.

"Hey, girly!" the older man exclaimed in English. "What you do there?"

She had put her whole palm against the screen. It flickered twice and went black with a final-sounding pop.

Hurriedly she grabbed for one of the little knobs at the bottom of the screen and began to fiddle with it furiously. "It started to flicker," she said. "Scan lines all over. But it went out before I could do anything." She turned to them with a shrug and her best helpless-little-girl smile.

She might not have known a lot about people, and especially their complex and irrational emotions. But she had learned early on some pretty significant manipulation skills.

The younger man jumped from his seat. "Could she have sabotaged it?"

"Relax," the older man said, playing the role of seasoned vet. "These sets are old. It must have burned out a tube. And anyway, if anything happens, it's not going to happen on that side of the platform!"

"LET IT ALL OUT," Tex said, killing the engine and unfastening his safety harness with calm dispatch. "It's good for the soul."

Annja had screamed like a teenage girl on a roller coaster. She didn't feel bad about it, either.

"Didn't you cut it a little close there?" she shouted.

He grinned back at her from outside in what was a pouring rain that bounced a good two feet off the steel decking. "Yep. What else are we doing here? Now, *move*."

"Couldn't they feel us hit?" she asked shakily as she clambered out.

A wave hit the rig and drenched the left side of her body. The platform, big as it was, shivered and swayed perceptibly. "Oh, my God!" Annja said.

"See, the storm turned out to be helpful after all," Tex said, reaching for the bag of armaments. "Given that we, you know, lived and everything."

They crouched uncomfortably on the seaward side of the plane, so that even if they were spotted their enemies wouldn't get a good look at them. It was a pretty weak reed, Annja knew, but she was just as willing to grasp at anything resembling advantage as Tex. She quickly stuffed spare magazines into the vest she had worn since takeoff from Papa Westray, a lifetime ago. The pistol rode in a spring-loaded break-front holster on her right hip.

"You don't mind, ma'am, I'll take this," Tex said, briefly hefting the shotgun. "You have the magical close-combat weapon."

Annja winced slightly at the term "magical." But she nodded.

"Wait here one," Tex said. Before she could assent or refuse, he was running bent over toward the helicopter parked forty yards south along the western edge of the platform. Annja crouched behind the ultralight, which had been spray-painted in irregular streaks of blue, gray and green. It seemed to break up the silhouette pretty well, and certainly didn't magnetize the eye the way the brilliant pristine white of the plane's original paint job had. She fleetingly hoped *Ariel* could be restored to her jovial and doting owner as good as new. Sadly, she doubted it.

A wave broke against the side of the platform and, as if in petty revenge for its inability to grab her and bear her back down to the depths, thoroughly soaked the back of her jeans.

"Great," she said aloud.

Tex came sprinting back, holding his slung shotgun with one hand to keep the butt from pounding him in the kidneys. "What was that about?" Annja shouted to him. Raising her voice seemed like poor noise discipline, but as a practical matter, she wasn't sure anybody would hear if Tex emptied the shotgun out here.

"Quick inspection." He jerked his head toward the superstructure, pierced irregularly by yellow lights. "Let's get going."

"SEE, I FIGURE I'm the Al Leong character," the young Asian sentry said in a California surfer-dude accent. His words echoed up the stairwell into which they had retreated in defiance of orders. They figured if they got caught their bosses would just have to understand. A North Sea gale changed everything.

His German partner grunted. He was a big burly guy with long, almost platinum-blond hair.

"Al Leong was in all these movies," the Asian kid went on. "He was always super cool. But nobody ever, like, recognized him. He was just an Asian guy with long hair and a mustache."

The German grunted.

"He never got any credit. He never got a shot at the big roles. It was total discrimination."

"Uh-huh," his partner said.

"But the other thing about Al Leong was, his character always got taken out first. You know, it's always the Asian dude who dies first. I figure that's why they hired me. I'm basically the canary in a coal—"

His words ended in a strangled noise. His partner turned to frown at him.

A fierce-looking woman was embracing the Asian kid from behind with an arm around his throat. The kid's eyes were rolling up in his head. Since that was plainly impossible, the German just stood a moment with his jaw falling slowly, trying to sort things back into proper order.

That was interrupted by a sharp impact to the rear of his skull and a shower of dazzling pyrotechnics. The world fell suddenly away from him.

"ARE THESE actually passive restraints?" Annja asked, kneeling on the young man's kidneys and trussing his wrists behind his back with a pierced plastic strip. She had let him down easy after choking him unconscious.

"Nope," Tex said. He already had the German's wrists secured, having expertly rabbit-punched him with the butt of his shotgun. "Just cable ties from Gannet. Don't fret—they'll work fine."

"I know who Al Leong is," Annja said. "I always liked seeing him in movies."

"I'm with you there," Tex said. "Even when he's wasted in something like *I Come in Peace.*"

"I liked that movie!"

As Annja stuffed a small wadded rag into her victim's slack-lipped, drooling mouth, Tex rolled the German onto his back. The man moaned. His eyes seemed to wander at random in their sockets. Tex grabbed the front of his pea coat and shook him. He barked a question in German. The guard moaned. Tex shook him again.

The German muttered something. Tex asked another question, received a sullen answer. Then he gagged the sentry and stood up. "What'd he say?" she asked. She was glad they hadn't had to kill these two. She also knew they were probably the last she and her partner could afford to extend deliberate mercy to. From this point on it was kill or be killed.

"He says there's at least twenty of their guys on the platform."

"Twenty?"

Tex shrugged. "Looks as if they got some operation going on here other than kidnapping teenage language geniuses. Speaking of which, he says your girl has a compartment of her own up on the top level. But she also has the run of the station. She could be anywhere."

"Great. Does that mean we have to check the place deck by deck, or whatever you call them?"

"Looks like it. We might as well check out the gangways first. If we start poking into all the compartments we'll raise the alarm pretty fast."

They both peered up the stairwell. They saw nothing but darkness. Safety standards did not seem to be foremost on the minds of the rig's current proprietors.

Annja followed Tex up the metal stairs past a tangle of huge pipes dimly lit by sporadic lamps placed by the people who occupied the derelict station. Both moved quietly, but it was probably effort wasted. Between the wind and the sea, the station moaned like a choir of the damned. The stink of petroleum and dead sea life was dense enough to make their eyes water and heads swim.

The first level up was dark. They paused on the railed-in landing outside as Tex peered through the little window in the metal door.

"You don't see in the dark, do you?" he asked her.

"No more than before all this started," she replied, feeling nettled without quite knowing why.

"We'll have to use our lights. Wish we could've got some night-vision gear. Oh, well. We got what we got. I'll use my light. Try to use yours as sparingly as possible, all right?"

"I know!"

He looked at her a moment, then grinned. "Sorry. Here I am lecturing you, and you're lots more current on doing this run-and-gun stuff than I am."

He went through the door. She slipped through after, easing it shut as noiselessly as possible. She felt bad for having snapped at him. He's helping me, she thought miserably, and here I am getting annoyed because he's good at it.

Tex advanced along the corridor holding his shotgun leveled at the waist by the pistol grip and the long sling around his neck. The little black flashlight he held in his raised left hand was shining out the bottom of his fist.

Holding her penlight unlit in her left hand, she followed. She left the pistol in its holster. Instead, after a moment's hesitation, she summoned the sword. She was comfortable with it. And it was quiet.

Both sides of the passageway had doors. One on the right opened quickly and quietly just after Tex, about a dozen feet ahead of Annja, passed by.

A man stepped out, aiming a black submachine gun at Tex's back.

16

Annja slashed the man with the machine pistol across the back. He uttered a gargling scream and fell.

Light poured out from the open door. Tex wheeled. Annja was moving already, whipping around the door frame into the compartment where the gunman had emerged.

Another man in a stained undershirt and dark running pants sat blinking sleepily, his bare feet dangling off the edge of his bunk. His eyes grew wide when he saw Annja. He grabbed for a Beretta lying on a table nearby.

She lunged. The point of her sword passed

through his thick unshaved neck. He screamed briefly as his blood splashed against the bulkhead. In the light of a lamp clamped to the bunk it was a blaze of scarlet against shades of gray.

Annja yanked the weapon free. The man slumped.

Tex was just rising from squatting beside the body of the first man as she emerged into the passageway. He held the dead guard's weapon. He offered it to Annja. "Walther MPL," he said. "Nine millimeter. Controls are pretty standard. Can you use it?"

She took it with her left hand. She intended to keep the sword in her right. Turning the Walther on its side, she found the charging lever and the safety.

"I think so," she said. "Thanks. Gives me a little better punch than the pistol."

"Thank *you*," Tex said with a quick grin. "Reckon I owe you one." He took his shotgun in both hands and led off again down the corridor.

The levels above were better lit. They moved through them rapidly but warily, but saw no one. If there were really over twenty people aboard the platform they weren't walking the hallways. Then again, the rig was big—bigger even than Annja had anticipated. Clearly deep-sea drilling was a complex, demanding operation, requiring much by way of both room and personnel.

As they reached the second-highest level a door opened and Jadzia popped out right in front of them.

Her eyes went wide. Then she hit Annja in a flying arms-and-legs hug that almost bowled the older woman backward off her feet.

"Annja! You came!"

"Of course," Annja said, blinking. She held her sword gracelessly away from her side. It was just luck the young prodigy hadn't impaled herself on it.

"What took so long? I saw you land—"

The door to the compartment she'd left opened, and a skinny, unshaven guy with a rat's nest of dark hair emerged. "Girl, why you go so quick?" he was asking in a dense accent, sounding more perplexed than suspicious.

That changed when he saw Jadzia clinging to a tall, striking woman holding a broadsword.

He opened his mouth to shout. Tex, moving with speed even Annja found remarkable, skipped in and butt-stroked him across the side of the head with his shotgun. He may have intended to be merciful, or merely to avoid rousing the dead with a shotgun blast echoing through the vast steel structure.

The man reeled back into the open doorway, clutching his head. Blood streamed from a split in his forehead and ran in rivulets down the back of his hand.

Then he began to jerk and writhe as automatic gunfire snarled from behind him. Bullets punched through the far door and bounced off the far wall to tumble whining down the corridor.

Annja took Jadzia to the floor beneath her to protect her from the ricochets. The girl cried out in alarm as the young man slumped into the corridor. From the way he went down it was clear he wouldn't get up again.

The head-hammering racket went on and on. Then suddenly it cut off.

Tex had gone down, too. He lunged to a crouch and spun around the side of the open door, shouldering the shotgun.

Inside the security room an older man was trying to cram a fresh magazine into a little black Skorpion machine pistol.

Tex fired twice. One charge, the shot still a tight column, smashed and all but severed the man's right forearm. The other punched through his sternum. He fell back, flailing wildly. The Skorpion cracked the screen of a monitor, which imploded with a pop.

As the ringing faded from Annja's ears she heard a siren begin to wail somewhere. It seemed to vibrate in the steel bones of the structure around her, setting up sympathetic resonances in her own skeleton.

"Time to go," Tex said, straightening. He leaned over, offering a hand to the women.

Annja sprang up. Jadzia likewise spurned the outstretched hand in favor of another surprising leap that wrapped him up in her long, surprisingly strong arms and legs.

"Tex Winston!" she cried. "I love your show! You really are an action hero!"

She planted a huge fervent smooch on his lips. He squirmed his face to the side. "I'm gonna be one dead action dude if we all don't get a move on!" he managed to get out as the girl smothered him with kisses.

Annja stood by scowling thunderously. Twenty feet along a door opened and a shaved head with a dark-bearded face poked out. Annja raised the Walther and sprayed bullets down the corridor. The head snapped back and the door banged shut.

Clutching Jadzia with one hand and the Benelli with the other, Tex started to stagger clumsily down the corridor. Annja slipped past him to take the lead.

As she reached the stairwell they had left, she heard Tex apologetically disentangling himself from Jadzia, who kept bubbling about what a huge fan she was and how he was so much more handsome in person.

The girl really needs to be slapped, Annja thought.

Annja slung the Walther to open the door, then unlimbered it and used the barrel jutting from beneath the gas cylinder to hold the door open. The first thing she heard was shouts, followed by footsteps. They were coming up.

"This way may be blocked," she shouted back. Tex was trying to fend off a renewed assault from Jadzia as delicately yet as decisively as possible. Annja realized the emotional reaction to being rescued had pretty well unbolted all the young woman's inhibitors. Of which she had not many to begin with.

"Where does the other door lead? Jadzia! Snap out of it," Annja ordered.

She put an edge in her voice that brought Jadzia's head around as if she actually had been slapped. "Stairs up to top level, and down to engine and generator room." She was flushed and breathless, and also dropping articles, which Annja had never heard her do. Usually she spoke English better than Annja.

"Engines?" she asked. "I thought the platform was supposed to stay put."

"For the drills," Tex said. "Hey—"

Annja was already sprinting past him and Jadzia. From the way she'd seen him handle himself, the rumors he had seen combat were likely true, but she was stronger, quicker and generally more lethal than he was. He knew it, too. But his gallant-cowboy self-image would make him uncomfortable letting her go into danger first. So she didn't hang around to discuss it.

She yanked the door open with her left hand, shook the Walther sling down her arm, grabbed the pistol grip and plunged into the stairwell.

A voice exploded in her left ear. She wheeled. A beefy crew-cut blond guy in a black ribbed pullover was almost on top of her, holding some kind of assault rifle. She slashed him across the face.

He fell back into the black-clad legs of the man following him down from the top deck. That man sat down hard against the stairs, cursing in hoarse French. Curses turned abruptly to screams. The hapless first man's blood and brain matter had just poured into his partner's lap.

She swatted the French man hard on the side of the head with her sword, stunning him to silent slackness.

That minor mercy did not extend to his fellows pounding down the stairs after him. She directed a quick burst up the stairs, into the shins of the next man. He fell backward, howling louder than the Frenchman. Annja blasted more bullets up the stairs into the dark. The reports were so loud in the metal stairwell that she felt the pressure on her eyeballs. Shouting men retreated rapidly upward.

"I got it!" Tex shouted, barging into the landing behind her. "Go!" Covering the stairs with the Benelli in his right hand, he hunkered down and relieved the dead sentry of his rifle.

From below, Annja heard more voices hollering at each other in apparent confusion. Then more footsteps pounding up fast.

17

Annja raced down at full speed to confront a group of heavily armed men charging up the steps. She slashed crosswise as a man turned toward her. He fell back with blood spraying from his belly.

She cut down two more men. The others turned and ran before her, down onto the engine-room floor, off among the enormous shadowed bulks of engines like dormant Titans.

From the room's far side a big yellow muzzle flare winked at her. Bullets cracked and keened around her, sparking off the railing. She dashed for the cover of what looked like some kind of chest-high control panel. She shrugged the

Walther's sling off again, caught the pistol grip and fired a burst toward where she thought the shots had come from.

She ducked down behind the panel. The thin-gauge metal would provide little protection against rifle or even jacketed pistol bullets, although if there was some kind of solid mechanism inside it would give some cover. It did conceal her from view, however, and that was something.

Shots crashed and echoed, the bangs seeming to grow in volume as they dropped in tone, filling the huge, mostly empty space. Muzzle-flashes lit the machinery around her in otherworldly yellow flickers. No bullets came near her.

A shotgun boomed from above. She wasn't sure what real chance Tex had of hitting anyone at that range. She heard the spatter of rubber soles on pierced steel decking, and turned to see Jadzia running up on her from behind. Long arms and legs were flailing everywhere. It was gangly and wasted lots of energy, but the girl did get some velocity, Annja thought.

"Come on," she said. She put the sword away in its special place to snatch Jadzia's thin wrist and

tow her at a full sprint toward a giant semicircu-
lar housing that rose from the floor twenty feet
away. It looked like a colossal casting of some
kind. It also looked as if it would shrug off a big
hit.

Bullets cracked at the heels of Jadzia's tennis
shoes. If her run had been uncoordinated before,
it was now totally out of control. It was all she
could do to keep her feet more or less beneath
her, as fast as Annja was pulling her along.

Annja turned to let her back slam against the
hard housing. Jadzia cannoned into her, squash-
ing her breasts uncomfortably and knocking her
breath out of her.

Tex came running and firing the shotgun. He
slammed up against the steel housing next to
Annja and began feeding fat plastic shells into
the Benelli from a pocket of his vest.

"You can *move*," he told Annja approvingly.
She noticed he had the recovered rifle slung
barrel-down behind his own left shoulder.

"You have spare magazines for that?"

He nodded. "Oh, yeah. Twenty rounds each,
7.62 mm NATO ball. Full-length rounds.

None of this underpowered assault-rifle stuff. Hoo-ah!"

"Good." She stepped past him, leaned out to fire off the last of the rounds in the magazine of her own scavenged machine pistol. To her dismay there were only two.

She tossed the weapon aside. "Keep their heads down," she said.

Before he could respond she gathered herself and climbed straight to the top of the housing, a dozen feet above the deck.

A shot cracked out from right beneath her, sharper than the 12-gauge's boom and a lot more authoritative than a 9 mm weapon. Tex was doing what she asked.

She jumped. Nearby a house-sized motor hunched, long dormant and now probably rusted beyond repair. She caught its upper edge with her hands and pulled herself onto the top. It's not too hard if you don't let yourself think about it, she thought.

She clambered through the musty dark, picking her way carefully across chill, slick metal and between tangles of conduit and cable. Icy water dripped down her neck. Outside the storm howled. The platform rocked continuously to its blows. Below her a firefight raged. By the sounds, Tex was augmenting aimed shots from his borrowed battle rifle with handgun rounds and even the odd shotgun blast, to conserve his limited stock of 7.62 mm ammo and perhaps to give the guards the impression they faced more intruders than they did.

Annja scrambled up a twisted conduit thick as her thigh, grabbed a dangling cut cable and swung up to a catwalk. She felt a strange sense of disconnection, of unreality. Am I really here, doing this? How did that happen, exactly?

The catwalk led her to the vast compartment's far wall. Ahead and to her left muzzle-flashes strobed from an oblong of brightness. It took her a moment to recognize the gray light of the storm and sunset outside, assisted by some back-scatter from a spotlight.

She selected a cable bundle running along overhead, summoned her sword and hacked through it. She winced, half expecting a blast of electricity to flash-cook her arm and knock her from her perch in a final fatal spasm. She knew the platform occupants must have fired some of its powerful generators. But she'd heard and felt no motor hum in this room, immense as it was. She'd gambled the cables weren't hot.

It paid off. Unshocked, Annja moved quickly along the catwalk, cutting through the straps holding up the wire bundle she had severed. When she had freed enough, she ran back to the cable's full extent, caught a good grip with her left hand and leaped over the catwalk rail to swing down.

If I live through this, she thought as she whizzed down, I'll never make fun of bungee jumpers again—

The improvised Tarzan vine came out about ten feet shy of the deck. That proved about ideal. Annja swept down at an angle, out of the shooters' lines of fire. Her boot soles skimmed above the rain-washed metal. As she started to swing up again she let go.

A man stood just inside the door firing a short-barreled CAR-4 loudly from the shoulder. Her feet caught him in the left side and slammed him to the steel. He nicely cushioned her fall.

The man beside him spun, trying to bring an MP-5 to bear on her. Annja slashed down. The stroke severed his left arm a handspan below his shoulder. He dropped the machine pistol to concentrate on screaming and clutching at his stump in a futile attempt to stem the spray of blood from his severed brachial artery.

Quickly Annja moved out the door into the storm's full force. A tall, gaunt man with a pointed-looking shaved head and a dark beard pointed the barrel of a full-length M-16 at her. With no defense, she launched into a forward roll, right toward him. The rifle snarled a 3-round burst. She felt the heat, felt muzzle blast slapping her face and forehead, but oddly heard nothing. She came up onto her feet, knees bent, grasping her sword with both hands. She drove forward, twisting counterclockwise. The blade bit through the rifleman's belly to erupt out his back in a cloud of black spray.

A second man turned and ran, still holding his MP-5. With no hesitation Annja used her forward momentum to come up sprinting. She ran the man down through stinging rain and cut him down with a diagonal slash. She could not afford to let him find cover and his composure and shoot at her friends.

She looked around. She had been instantly drenched. The storm had struck Claidheamh Mór B hard and true. She guessed she had come out just south of the northeast corner of the rig. She took a few steps to her left until she could see around the superstructure to where Tex had tied plucky little *Ariel* to a landing on the platform.

At once she ducked back. She sensed movement, wheeled to face it. Tex and Jadzia were pelting toward her.

"Great job," Tex said, panting a little. Jadzia was looking everywhere at once with her blue eyes saucer huge.

"Good news," Annja told him. "We don't have to worry about flying out in this."

He turned his head to look at her with one quizzical eye. "And the bad news?"

"We can't fly out. There are guards swarming all over the plane."

"What?" Jadzia yelped. Her initial reaction of elation at being rescued, and then her not-quite-moored-to-the-real-world sense that this was all some fantastic action-flick adventure had begun to curdle in the cold blast of reality. Maybe she'd seen enough spilled blood to realize it was *real*. Annja hoped so.

"You mean we're trapped here? You were too stupid to have a backup plan?" Jadzia said.

"Oh, no," Tex said with indefatigable cheer. "We have a backup plan. It's pretty stupid, too, but it's not like we have much choice."

They sprinted east, toward the near edge of the platform. "I hate Plan B," Annja shouted through the storm.

Just barely over the din she heard shouts from behind as somebody spotted them.

"Given how iffy Plan A was," Tex said, "how good could Plan B be?"

Shots crashed as if challenging the thunder. Slowing just shy of the platform edge, Annja looked over her shoulder to see muzzle-flashes flicker from high up in the superstructure.

"Down the hatch," Tex told Annja. A rectangular opening railed on three sides was cut through the deck. A fixed steel ladder was just visible inside.

"Don't be a hero," she told him.

His response was to kneel, bring the G3 to his shoulder, sight briefly and squeeze off a hefty slamming shot. Annja looked up to see a figure fall over a railing on the third level.

She grabbed Jadzia by the wrist and propelled her toward the ladder. Then she pulled the girl's wet face close to hers.

"Follow me down as fast as you can," Annja said.

"But—"

"No buts. You mess around, you die."

She went down the ladder. Almost at once she felt Jadzia pattering down after her, for once obeying instructions. She became concerned about the girl treading on her fingers or even kicking her in the head in her excitement. A wave broke against a steel support pylon below with a crash. Spray soaked the legs of Annja's jeans like a blast from a fire hose. She gasped despite herself. It was cold.

"I hate this," she muttered.

"Beg pardon?" a voice called from just below her.

Annja hadn't dared to look down. In part

because she couldn't bear to see the awful storm surge leaping up at her like hungry orcas. In part because of a cold gut fear that was *all* she would see.

But now she looked to see the bearded porkpie face of Phil Dirt anxiously upturned from the midst of the Zodiac boat. The ample form of Vicious Suze stood beside him. Lanky Lightnin' Rod was folded at the tiller, fighting to keep the boat under some semblance of control, although they had wisely lashed a line onto the bottom of the steel ladder.

"So you got the poor dear captive bird," Suze said. "Lovely."

Jadzia stepped on Annja's hand. Biting back a curse, Annja moved around to the far side of the steel ladder to help hand Jadzia down to the waiting radio pirates. Then, hearing a crackle of gunfire from above, she looked up, worried.

Tex came sliding down the ladder, braking by hitting every fifth rung or so with his boots. "I held 'em up as best I could," he said, "but we'd better not hang around too long."

Annja let herself down in the boat. She

didn't even much resent the way Phil Dirt's broad hand cushioned her butt to help ease her entry into the bobbing boat. Maybe it was even necessary. Maybe.

Suze helped Tex down.

"Much obliged, ma'am," he said. His words came short and his breath whistled with asthma.

She glanced up, then stooped. Straightening, she raised a long implement to point almost straight upward from her shoulder. Annja just recognized it as a double-barreled hunting shotgun when both barrels went off with a giant flash and a tremendous sound that boomed around between the steel platform and the sea for what seemed like minutes.

From overhead Annja heard a scream. Then she had to sit down hurriedly as Phil cast off and Rod set the boat whining away into the brutal sea trailing a rooster tail of spray behind.

"That's our Suze," Phil shouted. "A dab hand with a fowling piece. Tally-ho!"

GUS MARSHALL AND Louis Sulin emerged into the rain in time to see several of their men finish releasing the lines that held the helicopter to the deck. Its big main rotors were already circling and picking up speed.

"Shit," Marshall said.

Scowling, Sulin raised a walkie-talkie and began speaking into it intently.

Marshall cupped his huge hand around his mouth and bellowed, "Stop! Stand away, there!"

The storm drowned out his voice. Or maybe his and Sulin's men were too eager to show their zeal to their somewhat precarious superiors. The white-and-blue chopper rose from the deck. Bravely it turned into the wind, tipped forward, and swept off skimming the waves in pursuit.

Within seconds it exploded in a ball of yellow flame that plunged like a comet into the sea.

ANNJA SAW THE FLASH reflect from a wave breaking in front of them and distressingly high over their heads. As the Zodiac flew up she looked back to see what appeared to be a giant yellow comet plunging into the sea.

"The helicopter!" Jadzia exclaimed.

Half-horrified, Annja looked to Tex. He had just taken a hit from his inhaler. He shrugged.

"Isn't that just bad guys all over?" he said in a squeaky voice. "Don't do maintenance for diddly."

18

"I still can't believe you eat like that and keep that slim figure," Tex told Annja with what sounded as much like envy as amusement.

Annja looked down at her plate and shrugged. It was piled high with smoked salmon, eggs, bacon and boiled potatoes. Back at the table she shared with Tex and Jadzia she had a plate full of fresh fruit slices.

"She's a superheroine," Jadzia said matter-of-factly. "She needs to eat super amounts." Her own plate wasn't exactly empty.

After the rescue the Gannet crew had taken the three back to Papa Westray airfield. There

Annja recovered the bag of scrolls, which she had left locked in the airfield safe. They then caught a small airplane Tex had chartered to fly up from mainland Scotland and carry them across the North Sea. They were checked into a Copenhagen hotel by midnight.

As she headed back to the table with her breakfast Annja's cell phone rang. It took her by surprise. Did Leo get my number somehow? she wondered. Tex had been on and off his phone all morning trying to mollify the owner of the ultralight plane they had abandoned on the drilling platform. While Annja felt sorry for the jovial former RAF test pilot, she didn't want to deal with him.

"Good morning." The voice that poured from her phone when she flipped it open and held it to her ear was British, all right. But instead of Leo's hearty country-squire tones it was plummy and more quietly cheerful. "Have I the pleasure of addressing Ms. Annja Creed?"

"Yes."

"I represent the principal in a certain negotiation in which you took part, and which you recently broke off in a most precipitous manner.

You are to be congratulated for the pluck with which you carried that out, by the way. In its way, it was most admirable."

"Thank you," Annja said, trying to keep emotion out of her voice. She was glad she was sitting down so her knees didn't give out.

"What's wrong?" Tex asked, noticing the color drain from her face. She waved him to silence.

"We would like to parlay," the voice said. "Tête-à-tête, so to speak. If you are interested, please come alone on the Metro to the Radhusplads. A car will collect you. Your safety, your safe return and the safety of your associates while you are absent from them are all guaranteed."

"Why should I trust you?" Her fear hadn't quite evaporated, but only wisps remained. If they're bargaining, she thought, they no longer take for granted they can swat us whenever they please.

"Because you have something we want very badly," the voice said unflappably. "And we have paid the penalty for underestimating you. Once bitten, twice shy, my dear."

"DON'T GO," Tex and Jadzia said simultaneously when she recounted the conversation to them in an undertone. The restaurant was well peopled with tourists, loudly chattering in mostly accents of English, but not so crowded anyone was sitting near them.

"Not alone, anyway," Tex added.

The corners of Annja's mouth whitened ever so slightly as her lips compressed. She ducked her head to her coffee cup to hide the grimace, slight as it was. Despite—or maybe even because of—the gratitude she felt for Tex going to such lengths and taking such risks to help two near total strangers, she still felt abashed by how much she had needed to depend upon him. Even perhaps a touch resentful of his easy, self-assured competence.

She knew that was silly.

Annja tried to hide her discomfort with a laugh. "They reminded me we have something they want," she said. "And they know what a bad idea it is trying to hold one of us as hostage."

Jadzia sighed and scowled ferociously. "So then they maybe just kill you to frighten us," she said. "Stupid."

MAYBE JADZIA WAS RIGHT, Annja thought, watching downtown Copenhagen slide by outside the tinted windows of the limousine. When she emerged into the late-morning sunlight from the city's main underground station into the expanse of City Hall Square, the car slid smoothly to the curb right before her as if timing her arrival. It was a normal-looking limo, a modestly stretched white Mercedes with dark gray interior. The young blond man in the gray uniform and cap who popped out the driver's side to open the rear passenger door for her was polite, even quietly affable.

All the same she checked the inside of the door to ensure it was no trap before she let him close it on her. It had a handle. The chauffeur resumed his place, and the car glided smoothly forward, sending a flock of fat pigeons flapping up into a pale blue sky whisked with white clouds.

The central square was half surrounded by quaint old buildings flanking the city hall itself and half by somewhat dingy looking modern glass-and-concrete boxes. The limo left it quickly behind. What she saw of the city as a whole consisted of older buildings interspersed with relatively few and smallish skyscrapers.

The car made several turns and approached a great gleaming spear that resembled a Gothic cathedral faced in green glass, whose topmost mast threatened to snag the clouds. It had a newness and a brashness about it. And more than a little arrogance—it seemed by far the tallest building in the city.

The car stopped in front of it. A man strode from the covered entryway. As the chauffeur helped Annja out he approached, beaming with white horsey teeth out of a dark face and extended a hand that seemed to consist entirely of knuckles.

"And you are the most charming Ms. Annja Creed," he said in the ripe voice she had heard on the phone. By his tone, meeting her was the thrill of his entire year if not his life. He took her hand, bent low, kissed it with dry lips.

"I am Mr. Thistledown," he said. Despite the Jeeves accent he looked Middle Eastern to Annja, possibly Turkish. His dark suit was double-breasted and immaculate. He had cheeks like doorknobs and big dark eyes that sparkled with some secret amusement. Though she guessed he was in his fifties his hair was dark, thinning slightly and slicked back. It might have been dyed. "So good of you to join us."

"I'm charmed, Mr. Thistledown." Which was at least colorably true, so far as he personally was concerned. His charm did not persuade her to forget for whom he worked, nor to trust him.

He escorted her into the building, chatting about the weather. She tuned him out, contenting herself to nod and make occasional polite noises and only paying enough heed to ensure she didn't agree to anything outrageous. The building was modern, all mirror-polished red marble, enormous sprays of tropical fronds and a profusion of gleaming chrome. Soft ambient music flowed from concealed speakers. The air smelled faintly of forest, apparently to reinforce the corporate image of almost painful ecoconsciousness.

A discreet door to one side of the lobby opened to a private express elevator. As it rose it proved to have glass walls. Rising past the three-story height of the atrium-like lobby she found herself on the outside of the building, rising as if on a magic carpet.

She checked Thistledown surreptitiously. He did not seem to be scrutinizing her for signs of fear of heights. Nonetheless she took for granted the elevator was designed to intimidate anyone who rode in it for the first time.

Despite the smiling faces of every Euro Petro employee she had encountered, she couldn't help noticing a fairly subtle intimidation was a force in the company's physical manifestations.

"You are a most remarkable woman, Ms. Creed," Thistledown said. He smelled faintly of lavender. "You have made quite an impression on Herr Direktor Sinnbrenner."

"Who?" she asked, a beat belatedly.

The smile widened. His eyeballs were slightly yellow, suggesting to her somehow that the flawless white teeth were dentures.

"Dieter Sinnbrenner," he said, "our chief operations officer."

She felt the elevator begin to decelerate as a sense of lightness. It stopped. The brushed-brass doors slid open. Thistledown gestured outward with a large hairy hand. It comported oddly with the dark coat sleeve and crisp white shirt cuff from which it sprang.

"Herr Direktor," he said, "please allow me to introduce Ms. Annja Creed. Ms. Creed—"

For a moment Annja thought the penthouse was under construction. It seemed to be entirely bare and open to the surrounding sky. Then she realized that like the elevator it had total-window walls, except for the housing of the elevator itself. A surprisingly modest desk sat near the far wall, offset to her right.

A man with a full head of silver hair stood with his back to Annja, gazing out the windows. The daylight streaming in silhouetted him so completely she could make out no detail of his appearance except the hair and dark suit. He bounced once on his heels and turned.

"Excellent," he said in crisply accented English. "Thank you, Mr. Thistledown."

Annja stepped forward onto a dark carpet. The doors hissed shut behind her. She realized her escort had stayed in the elevator.

The man strode forward extending a hand. To Annja's surprise his face was narrow, handsome and unlined as a twenty-five-year-old's. His eyebrows were carbon-black. Only when he drew near did she realize he was at least four inches shorter than her. He had a huge presence.

"Believe me when I say it is a very great pleasure to meet you, Ms. Creed," he said.

After the briefest of hesitation she took his hand. She felt that if she acted rude by refusing the handshake, she would somehow sacrifice the moral high ground. She did half hope he would try some kind of hand-crushing game. The hope was in vain. His grip was strong and dry and exactly metered.

"I have to admit I find that hard to believe, Herr Sinnbrenner," Annja said coldly.

He smiled and his age showed around the brown eyes. The skin was scored deeply at the corners, as if he had spent his life staring into blinding sunlight.

"How do you find our quarters?" he asked, pacing rapidly several steps away from her.

"Imposing," she said. "As I'm sure they're intended to be. But also surprising."

He turned back. He had a curious stop-and-go quickness to his movements, suggesting at once a machine and a lizard.

"How so, please?"

"Looking around the Copenhagen skyline it appears pretty evident they have ordinances regulating maximum building height," she said. "Which this building obviously exceeds."

He smiled again, like a camera shutter flicking. "We represent the majesty of the European Union, after all. We are exceptional, candidly. Exceptions, accordingly, are made."

He turned precisely and paced a few steps to her left. He stopped as if expecting a response. Then he shook his head once sharply. "But I waste your time with rhetoric. Let me come directly to the point. You have something. We want it. What is your price?"

"What makes you think I'd deal with you at any price," she said, "after what you pulled with my friend?" Under the circumstances, labeling the still-difficult Jadzia her friend seemed an acceptable white lie.

He rolled a hand palm upright. "Self-interest. Consider the carrot and the stick."

She inhaled sharply. "I'll make a counteroffer. We keep the scrolls and continue to conserve them properly and extract their meaning using proper scientific procedures. You keep off our backs."

He raised a brow. "And what is in this bargain for us?"

"Self-interest," she said. "All these assaults and kidnappings and murders must have cost you."

For a moment his self-control flickered. He stared at her with hatred so undiluted she felt it as a psychic blow. "Exceedingly so," he hissed.

He turned away and walked toward the window. He clasped his hands behind his narrow waist and bounced rapidly up and down on the balls of his feet three times.

"But a tiny fraction of what lies at stake here," he said to the city beneath him. "You have no idea." He half turned toward her. "You have your lives to consider, Ms. Creed. Think well on that."

"I've thought of little else since your murderers attacked my innocent friends in Alexandria," she said.

I could do it, she thought. It would be so easy. An exertion of will. A few quick steps. A swing. Yet she could not bring herself to cut him down in cold blood.

"Also, I don't trust you, Herr Direktor," she said. "You can take your carrot and stick it where the sun don't shine."

He nodded, unfazed. "As you wish, my dear."

He faced back squarely out toward the heart of the great city. His attitude seemed to be not that of one who owns everything he sees, but of one who has just created everything he sees and is critically scrutinizing it to see if he finds it good.

The elevator doors hissed open behind her. She only just managed to catch control of herself before she leaped into the air spinning like a startled cat. She still turned more quickly than she wanted to.

Mr. Thistledown stood beaming at her from inside the car. "Ms. Creed, if you will?"

To her relief he maintained a smiling silence

on the long ride down. Annja stood with her nose close to the transparent outer wall and splayed hands just touching it. The glass felt cool to her fingertips. Her mind registered nothing beyond it.

She did notice when the lower levels of the tower rushed up to envelop them. She turned to face inward.

On the trip up she had been so taken by surprise by her surroundings she had not noticed that a mezzanine ran around the upper half of the ground floor. Two men stood by the railing. One was huge and bearlike and wore a suit that looked as if it had been stamped out of cardboard. The other was slim and neat as a ferret in a long off-white jacket and trousers, with fine features and unruly white hair.

From Jadzia's description she recognized the chief kidnappers, Gus Marshall and Louis Sulin. Smiling, she waved at them.

One minute later, when Marshall and Sulin came racing out the front of the building in pursuit of Annja, she was nowhere to be seen.

When the limousine had approached the Euro Petro tower Annja made a note of underground stops close to it. A short sprint took her into one of them the moment she left the building. There was little enough foot traffic in the immediate vicinity that she could accomplish it without jostling anyone and drawing unwanted attention to herself.

Once down in the cool but well-lit station she laughed out loud. There enameled in tile on the wall was a sign clearly announcing the next stop lay beneath the city hall building itself. The rendezvous at Radhusplads and the limo ride had been nothing but theater.

She trotted up the steps of a terrace to a side entrance of the hotel. The air blew crisp and smelling pleasantly of saltwater off Øresund, the sound separating Denmark from Sweden, which the hotel overlooked.

She trotted up three flights of stairs to the floor where she shared a room with Jadzia right next door to Tex. It wasn't so much that she felt the need for exercise. It was more that she seldom saw a point in slowing herself by taking elevators. Especially if she had the stairs to herself.

She was just about to swipe her electronic key through the lock when Tex's door flew open. Jadzia stormed out. Her face was purple and she was crying with huge sobs that racked her slender frame—which was wrapped in a towel.

Tex came right out behind her, dripping wet, wearing a fuzzy white hotel bathrobe. He halted when he saw Annja. Their eyes met.

Jadzia had the opportunity then to condemn Tex irredeemably in Annja's eyes in spite of all he had risked and all he had done for both women. But her lack of people skills betrayed her.

"I am not good enough for you, is that it?" she screamed at Tex. She batted at him with tight-clenched fists. "You don't want me?"

He had an undecipherable look on his face. Jadzia drummed her fists against his chest. "I hate you," she said, no longer screaming, but with baleful intensity. *"I hope you die."*

For a moment everyone froze and held a tableau. Jadzia went pale, as if her words had managed to penetrate her armor of self-centeredness deeply enough to shock even herself.

With a child's broken sob she spun away, clutching at the towel. Annja just had time to swipe the lock of the room they shared and pull the door open before the girl bolted face first into it. She vanished inside.

Tex was shaking his head. He looked as if he wanted to cry. "I didn't mean to hurt her feelings," he said. He ran a hand through his wet, spiky hair. "She just kinda caught me by surprise, slipping into the shower with me the way she did. I'm afraid I didn't handle that any too gently."

"She had it coming," Annja said with a notable lack of compassion. "Did she use that weird death-to-electronics trick of hers to burn out your room lock?"

"Huh? Oh, no. Those're designed to fail-safe. They lock if they go out, and won't open except from inside until they're reset. No, she talked the room maid into letting her in. In the lady's native Turkish."

19

"Joey," Tex called, settling his gray-and-maroon flight bag farther back over his left shoulder and striding forward into the bright southeast Texas sunlight. "Joey Travis! Great to see you, compadre."

As Tex embraced a short, dark-haired guy in an army jacket, Annja staggered slightly. It wasn't because she carried the hefty bag of scrolls, as well as her own duffel, despite Tex's periodic gallant attempts to relieve her of the burden. But the sun's dazzle almost stopped her in midstride. The cantilevered awning in front of the tall glass-paneled facade of the George

Bush International Airport kept the direct late-morning sun off but did nothing about the blinding reflection from the pickup lane and the cars jostling for position in it. The air hit her like a wet blanket. The humidity was no worse than in Copenhagen, perhaps, but springtime was already hot season here on Buffalo Bayou, a long spit from Galveston Bay and the Gulf of Mexico. She smelled petroleum and hot asphalt.

"Come and meet the ladies, Joey," Tex said, bringing his friend forward with an arm around his shoulder. "Joey, meet Annja Creed, archaeologist extraordinaire and sometime talking head on our friendly rival show, *Chasing History's Monsters*. And Jadzia Arkadczyk, who despite her youthful appearance is an internationally recognized heavy hitter on the subject of ancient languages."

"Hey, girls," Joey said.

"*Women,*" Jadzia said. She snapped her gum.

Still, the look in her blue eyes was calculating in a way that made Annja nervous. Delayed adolescence and hormones seemed to be rearing their ugly heads again.

"Sure," Joey said with a smile. He was thin and quick in his motions, with a face hollow enough in the cheeks Annja wondered if it resulted from poor nutrition rather than genes or fitness. His eyes were hazel with unusually long lashes. His hair was brown and retreating ever so slightly to either side. He had a couple days' growth of beard on his sunken cheeks. He seemed never to stay entirely still.

"Pleasure to meet you," he said.

Annja decided to give him the benefit of the doubt, and greeted him pleasantly. His grip was strong and firm but quite quick, as if he shied from contact.

Annja took over Jadzia's bag along with her own and the scrolls. She wanted a pretext to go around to the rear gate of the gray-and-white battered Jeep Grand Cherokee to share a quick word with Tex while Joey, all gallantry, helped Jadzia into the rear seat of the vehicle.

"He seems kind of anxious," she said softly, "your friend does."

Tex heaved his bag inside on top of a jumble of what looked like camping gear and drab olive groundsheets and, without asking, peeled Jadzia's bag away from Annja's left shoulder.

"He's just wound a little tight," he said, putting the girl's luggage in the hatch with considerably more care than his own. "Always been that way. Doesn't mean much. He managed to get through jump training and Ranger school with me."

A shadow crossed his face like a small cloud passing the sun. He smiled and relieved Annja of her own bag. She let him. She put the bag of ancient scrolls carefully inside.

Tex slammed the hatch shut. "Time to go."

TEX HAD THOUGHT he might know who could be of help to Annja and Jadzia in their quest and it came down to Joey Travis. Not on his own account so much as that of his uncle, Amon Hogue. Carthage Oil and Gas was a major second-tier U.S. oil concern. Annja wasn't sure whether he was chairman or president or CEO. All Tex or Joey would say was that Hogue *was* CO and G.

Tex and Joey sat in the front seat chatting amiably like two good ol' boys. No matter how much Massachusetts-born Idaho cowboy Winston hated his nickname, he could definitely pass for Texan. Then again, having seen him in action, Annja reckoned he could probably pass about as well in a Mumbai slum or an Atshuara village in the Upper Amazon watershed. He had a knack for fitting in and getting along. It made her feel insular and withdrawn, as if her psyche and her choices were constrained in some kind of thin glass bottle.

Jadzia leaned forward between the seats with her chin on folded arms, chewing gum and affecting fascination with a conversation she almost certainly would find stupid if Annja took part in it.

Annja glanced out the window at a semi headed the other way with a giant green bulldozer chained on the flatbed trailer and drummed her fingers on the cracked top of the door panel. A half dozen Gold Wing bikes roared past them in the fast lane.

Joey followed the Beltway bypass around where it curved south and ran along the west side of the Sheldon Reservoir, then turned east on the Beaumont highway that ran past the reservoir's south end. Every now and then they came across a single working oil rig of the kind Annja always thought of as "dickey bird," bobbing incessantly for black gold, sometimes literally in someone's backyard.

As they came up on what a sign identified as the San Jacinto River, Jadzia let out a yip like a pup with its tail stepped on.

She pointed right. Annja looked to see, south of the bridge and on the river's far side, a collection of towers, scaffolding and white-painted pipes of a sizable oil refinery. Above it rose a white oval sign with a big blue EP logo.

Annja felt gut-punched.

"What?" Tex asked, turning around. Annja nodded toward the refinery.

"Whoa," he said. "Is that new?"

"Uh-huh," Joey said. "They bought out an American company a year or so ago. They're moving hard against the smaller companies. That's one of the reasons I'm sure my uncle will want to help you."

"I hope you're right," Annja said. It still sounded like a long shot—that Amon Hogue would be willing to use his power and influence to help them get more of the scrolls transcribed. Although Hogue was relatively small as players of the global oil game went, according to Internet sources his net worth hovered around $850 million. It was hard to think of eighty-five percent of a billionaire as small, but Annja realized the game was very large indeed.

What exactly the Texas tycoon—who was known for his fondness for fast horses, young women and old whiskey—might do to help them she also had no clue. On the other hand his kind of money could buy a lot of options.

"Are we in Louisiana yet?" Jadzia asked after they had been driving for some time. A big flight of cattle egrets lifted from a stretch of water winding sluggishly away to the southwest.

"Uh-uh," Tex said. "Still in Texas. Not planning on leaving, at least until we've talked to Uncle Amon."

They crossed the Trinity River, turned north up State Highway 140 at a town called Liberty. At a wide patch of road called Moss Hill they turned right. A mile or so past the turnoff to the

Loblolly Unit of the Big Thicket National Preserve, Joey turned north onto an unmarked dirt road. It wound through alternating stands of pine, scrub oak and sweetgum for what Annja thought was at least a mile before Joey pulled off onto a wide spot in the road beside a bayou.

A little weathered wood shack stood there, the appearance of timelessness spoiled a little by a gas pump and a lot by the satellite dish on the roof.

"This is our stop, ladies," Joey said, killing the engine. "Better get your gear. Uncle Amon might want to spirit you away somewhere. Like a safehouse or something."

"A *safehouse,*" Jadzia breathed. Her eyes glittered. She was clearly enjoying the cloak-and-dagger aspects of their journey.

More than Annja, anyway. As she hefted the scrolls from the opened back of the Cherokee she caught Tex's eye and arched an eyebrow. He shrugged. "I don't know what happens next," he said. "I guess all we can do is cross our fingers and keep moving."

Annja had no better idea to offer. Tex handed

Jadzia's bag to her as Annja shouldered her own. Then they followed Tex to the dock. A white-haired black man wearing denim coveralls sun-faded and grease-stained to a sort of brown-and-white tie-dye stood talking to Joey. Beyond them a curious contrivance like a low platform with a big openwork cage at one end sat on top of some yellowing weeds flattened on the bank.

"What is that?" Jadzia asked, sounding a little dubious for the first time.

"An airboat?" Annja said incredulously.

Tex shrugged. "They got bayous," he said. "I guess they can have airboats."

"We use 'em a lot around here," Joey called. "All right, Vearle. We'll take it from here."

"You take care of yourself out there, Joey," Vearle said. To the others he waved, then shuffled back inside as if his feet hurt.

The boat sported a big airplane-style propeller with eight blades enclosed in the cage. In front of it was mounted what looked like a car engine. Before that a single bucket seat, built up about three feet above the hull with a long lever, evidently a tiller, to the right of it was obviously a driver's seat. Two bench-style seats were set in front of it, both facing forward.

Tex and Joey stashed the bags in a space under the operator's seat and pulled a blue synthetic groundsheet over them to protect them from spray and, Annja guessed, oil seepage from the engine. The water smelled of tannin and rotting vegetation. Minute flies or gnats swarmed around them. Fortunately they weren't the biting kind.

Joey helped the two women into the boat. Tex sat down beside Annja. Jadzia took the seat in front of them. Annja recalled a time when she'd always wanted to ride in the front on roller coasters. She didn't do that anymore. She didn't feel much desire to ride roller coasters at all. Her life had become enough of a thrill ride by itself.

Joey climbed in last, clambered up into his seat and fired up the engine. It roared and pushed the boat down the couple of yards to the bayou, throwing up a swirl of debris behind. The boat splashed and wallowed a little as it entered the water. Joey turned the square prow northwest.

The engine noise rose to a howl and the small craft shot forward with an exhilarating rush.

They passed a stand of trees killed and silvered by a fire and partially swallowed by the bayou, then made their way through a half-drowned forest of living oak trees. The bayou bent east. A big gleaming white structure appeared ahead on the right as they followed the curve.

Out front stood a big well-kept wooden dock with a boathouse. With a flourish Joey turned the airboat and ran it up on the bank next to the dock, flattening the long grass beneath. When he killed the engine the silence fell like a blow.

Leaving the other bags, Annja retrieved the scrolls. Jadzia offered to carry them. Annja was a little surprised. Jadzia hadn't shown much disposition to physical work. Then she realized the younger woman probably felt proprietary about the artifacts and wanted to associate herself with them in the near-billionaire's mind.

They walked up a white-graveled path with old railroad ties for sidings to the porch. The hunting lodge had a sprawling, comfortable

look. It was built of whitewashed wood with a
cypress shake roof. Some old pecan trees, not yet
coming into bloom, shaded the front and sides.

The porch boomed beneath their feet. Tex
held the door while Joey pushed ahead. Jadzia
went in after, then Annja. Tex came in last.

It was dark and seemed almost chilly. Annja
wasn't sure if there was air-conditioning or just
shade and contrast to the afternoon heat outside.
Her eyes adjusted slowly, becoming aware of a
calculated rustic-seeming interior. There was a
longhorn rack on a dark-stained wood plaque on
the wall above a fieldstone fireplace. Off to the
right of the door a large figure sat in a chair covered
in black-and-white cowhide. He faced away from
the newcomers, toward a giant plasma TV in one
corner of the room. He seemed to be asleep.

Joey took a step toward the seated figure.
"Uncle Amon?" he said, sounding uncertain.

A small, slim man with white hair, a white
tropical-weight silk suit and a lilac-colored tie
that matched his eyes emerged from a door on
the room's far side, and a shot rang out.

20

Annja sensed them around her—dark presences in the cool, dark front room of the lodge. Closing in from beyond her peripheral sight.

The pistol cracked again. It sounded very loud in the living room of the lodge. Tex rocked back just slightly to the second bullet's impact. The front of his blue denim shirt blossomed with a spreading stain. He went to his knees on the plank floor with a thump. His eyes rolled up in his head and he fell forward.

Jadzia screamed.

Annja felt as if her body had turned to ash inside her skin.

Joey gaped at his fallen friend. Beyond him Annja now saw that a big single-action revolver lay on the floor by the cowhide chair, near a hand that dangled over one arm. In a flash of comprehension she realized the tycoon had been suicided— subdued, possibly drugged, hand wrapped around grip, weapon held to temple and discharged.

"You said nobody'd get hurt!" Joey shouted. He turned and started toward his uncle.

A man wearing blue jeans and a stained gray work shirt stepped out from the same hallway from which Louis Sulin had emerged. He fired a pump shotgun from the hip. The blast was horrendously loud. The charge took Joey in the left kidney. He staggered, bending backward in agony, grabbing himself with both hands. The man racked the slide, shouldered the weapon and shot him in the head.

Sulin half turned. "Who told you—?"

Annja side-kicked him with all her strength.

She thought she felt something break, but even as she moved she had seen from the corner of her eye a man emerge from a door to her left holding a handgun. With no time to make sure of a killing blow, she had only been able to take

Sulin out of the action for at least a few moments.

Crying incoherently, Jadzia launched herself at the shotgunner. Whether taken by surprise or reluctant to shoot a woman, he never brought the weapon up before she started clawing and pummeling at his face. He pushed her away. She sat down hard on the floor.

He turned toward Annja, raising the shotgun. She was on him. The sword flashed side to side. The man was dead before he could understand what had happened.

Annja kept turning. A man loomed next to her right shoulder. He had been one of an unknown number who stood in ambush flanking the front door, out of immediate sight, poised in expectation that once Joey waltzed blithely in with his cheery greeting to his uncle, the others would follow without a care.

Carelessly. Just the way they did.

He seemed thunderstruck at the sword in Annja's hand. But he had a gun in his. Annja brought the blade up and then down, slashing him diagonally from left to right. He screamed and fell back against the wall with blood spraying from his chest.

Another man lunged at her. Annja cut upward. The man uttered a bubbling bellow and went to his knees with his guts slopping out of his ripped flannel shirt. She slashed another man across the eyes. As she did so he fired a handgun. The shot missed, but the flare dazzled her eyes. Unburned propellant thrown out by the blast stung her cheek.

An assailant threw down a Taurus double-action revolver and turned to run toward what seemed like the dining room, to the left of the front door. Annja slashed him across the back without remorse. He was a killer. The man pitched forward screaming and writhing. Instead of putting him out of his misery she jumped over him. His screams would distract his fellows and drain their morale. He was vivid evidence of the cost of trifling with Annja Creed and those under her protection.

Jadzia sat on the floor with her knees up, staring at everything with wild eyes. Annja put the sword away, grabbed up the shotgun Joey's murderer had dropped when she'd struck him and jacked the pump. She confirmed at least one more shell was in the tubular under-barrel magazine, then leaned around to blast one down the hallway.

Sulin lay slumped at the far end, feeling his ribs. He held his pistol in one hand. He rolled quickly out of the way as she fired. She was pretty sure she'd missed.

She worked the pump again, trying to remember how many shells a shotgun held. If it was a combat gun, as it seemed to be, she thought she recalled it would have a capacity of seven or eight.

Somebody came through the door to what she suspected to be the kitchen, at the other end of the big front room where Uncle Amon slumped in his chair of eternal repose. Annja shouldered the weapon, flash-sighted through the ghost ring, fired as he took up an isosceles stance pointing his Model 1911 .45 at her. The gunman's face crumpled in on itself as if punched in by an invisible fist—or a sledgehammer.

She looked at Jadzia again. The girl's face went red and started to knot up to cry as the first shock subsided. "No time," Annja said roughly. "Get up."

She took the girl's arm. Jadzia scrambled to her feet quickly enough, bringing the bag full of scrolls with her. Annja was relieved to see once again that when the hammer came down, Jadzia was willing to follow the lead of somebody experienced in real-time trouble.

Belatedly Annja pumped the shotgun, then moved to the kitchen side of the front door, keeping a wary eye on the door in the back of the room. "When I give the word," she told the girl, "I want you to throw the front door open hard. Don't go out. Understand?"

Jadzia nodded. Annja moved to the window. Some chintz curtains framed it, and a gauzy hanging masked the outdoors from clear view from inside—and vice versa.

Annja caught Jadzia's eye. The girl was weeping and biting her lip but seemed in control. "Now!"

Jadzia grabbed the latch, yanked the door open and gave the screen a kick. A startled exclamation rang out from just outside.

Shotgun in hand, holding her left arm protectively bent in front of her eyes, Annja jumped through the front window. The wood frame screeched and gave way. Glass exploded around her. She felt it clawing her like a bagful of angry wildcats.

She had no time to think about it. A man with a Mini-14 carbine stood with his back toward her. She summoned the sword and cut him down.

Another man had an assault rifle pointed into the open front door. Fortunately Jadzia had had the sense to jump aside after booting open the door. The man gaped at Annja and swung the rifle at her with the speed of pure adrenaline.

She lunged, thrust. The sword punched through his sternum, through his heart and lungs. His eyes went wide.

"Come on!" she shouted in the door. She heard voices from inside, as well as from around to the rear of the house.

Jadzia stumbled out carrying the scrolls. She was full-on crying, with great whooping sobs. "Tex," she moaned. "They killed him!"

"They'll kill us, too, if we don't move." Putting the sword away, Annja seized Jadzia's arm and led her half stumbling toward the airboat.

"Do you know how to drive this?" Jadzia asked, scrambling in. She seemed not so much to have stopped her crying fit as put it on hold as curiosity got the better of her.

"Not yet," Annja said. "Hold this."

She handed the shotgun to the girl, hoping it would distract her, hoping she'd have the sense not to shoot Annja, herself or the engine by accident.

A red button by the high driver's seat started the engine with a cough and a snarl when Annja stabbed it with her thumb. Evidently Joey had felt confident about leaving it unlocked in front of his uncle's grand hunting lodge. Joey had been confident about a lot of things that hadn't turned out so well.

She guessed the tiller worked in a fairly intuitive way. Push it left to go right, but no reverse lest the huge fan blow driver and passengers right out of the shallow skiff hull. She pushed the stick forward. The engine noise rose in pitch and the boat commenced to move.

She powered it around in a semicircle. That seemed to be the plan anyway, and it moved readily enough with the long moist grass as a sort of lubrication. Nothing ripped the bottom out of the airboat as it slewed about. The engine and fan were unbelievably loud in the driver's seat. Annja was suddenly much aware of the chopping power of those blades spinning a few feet behind her. The craft reached the water. Annja's heart almost stopped as the bow pushed down into it as if to break the surface and head straight to the bottom. Instead it bounced back and obediently lit out across the water.

She steered it back the way they had come. "Why are we going this way?" Jadzia yelled at her.

"We know there's a ride this way," she shouted. She didn't see any point in trying to lead the inevitable pursuit on a wild goose chase. She was willing to gamble Sulin would not yet have bothered sending men to secure Joey's Grand Cherokee. They had other priorities.

"Do you think they'll chase us?" Jadzia asked. Again she showed a tendency to snap out of it in actual danger, and lapse back into hysterics when things calmed down. While Annja could have done without any hysteria whatsoever, she was grateful it only came out when it did.

"I'd be amazed if they didn't," she replied.

"Here they come!" Jadzia screamed, pointing past the starboard edge of the fan cage.

The airboat swerved slightly as Annja turned her head. A big boat came powering around a bend in the bayou beyond the lodge. It pushed a big foam-edged wave of tea-colored water before it. Its wake threw dirty water across the dock.

A man in the powerboat's prow shouldered an M-16 and fired. She didn't see where the bullets went, wasn't sure if she'd even hear the cracks of their supersonic passage above her engine's howl. Two other men hung on the rail behind him holding long guns. Sulin wasn't there. Annja guessed she had busted some ribs for him.

Another burst ripped a line of miniature waterspouts past them on the right. Jadzia cried. Annja veered the boat starboard through the falling spray of the last one. A plan formed in her mind.

As she suspected, the next burst tore the water more or less along the line she had followed a moment before. She felt her gut tighten. The mass of the automobile-style engine would easily absorb the needle-like bullets—protecting her body. The engine would likely suck in a lot of them before it stopped running. But she feared a hit on one of the propeller blades would leave them literally dead in the water.

And shortly after that, just plain dead.

She began to weave the little craft back and forth across the bayou, which ran relatively broad. The powerboat's engine roared, audible above the airboat's own motor, surging in predatory pounce-reflex as its crew sensed vulnerable prey.

"Don't be stupid!" Jadzia screamed. "Quit swerving! It's catching us!"

"It's faster anyway," Annja called back grimly. Their only advantage was maneuverability—and with a drowned forest coming up even that would shortly be restricted. "Anyway, we can't outrun bullets."

To Annja's horror the girl stood up, pale legs braced, and fired the shotgun from the hip. She had presence of mind—or luck—enough to shoot on a turn so that the shot charge cleared Annja and even the wide sweep of the prop. But she hadn't anticipated the savage 12-gauge recoil, which Annja's old combat-shooting instructor had confided was almost impossible even for a strong, trained man to control effectively in rapid fire. The single blast was enough to tear the gun out of Jadzia's hands and knock her on her rump in the bilge. The shotgun fell overboard to vanish with a splash.

Annja hoped Jadzia hadn't hurt herself too badly. The girl seemed mostly stunned. As for the shotgun, it had formed no part of the plan flash-formed in Annja's mind anyway.

She heard the powerboat's roar grow louder. She threw the airboat broadside across its path. She chopped the throttle and let the engine die.

Annja could hear Jadzia's despairing wail as the airboat wallowed and stopped. It rode up on the great swell pushed before the onrushing powerboat's bow. Annja saw the men on deck, taken as fully by surprise as she had hoped, jostling to try to get to the port rail to shoot as the boat's driver swerved alongside the airboat.

As it did, Annja sprang. Time seemed to slow as she hung suspended in air between the craft. Then she caught the chromed rail with her left hand.

The impact almost wrenched the shoulder out of its socket. She twisted. Her hip slammed against the slick white hull. The sun-heated metal rail seared her palm.

A face stared over the rail at her, a comic mask of surprise, eyebrows arched, eyes and mouth ovals of astonishment. The man was holding a CAR-4 automatic carbine. Annja summoned the sword and thrust it up through the open mouth.

She felt a moment of resistance, a squishy sensation. He collapsed instantly to the deck as she pithed him like a frog. Six inches of blade protruded from the back of the man's head. The sword shone pristine, as if its metal refused to be sullied.

She got the soles of her shoes against the hull, using her legs, as well as her grip on the rail to vault onto the deck, which now ran pink. Her motion yanked the sword free on its own.

The other man who had stood behind the bow gunner swung his full-size M-16 in a clumsy attempt to club her. She easily fended off the lightweight weapon with her left hand. She slashed him diagonally across the chest, high right, down left, then took a return backhand cut across his belly.

As he fell screaming, the man in the bow aimed his long black rifle at Annja from his shoulder. She raced toward him, sword raised. As he fired she veered right, hacked across her body. The blade sliced through the M-16's receiver.

The shooter screamed as a cartridge, severed in midignition, vented furnace-hot gases into his face. She brought a short chopping stroke down on the left side of his forehead. His shrieking stopped. He toppled backward. She wrenched the sword free and he flopped backward over the rail like a fish released to the waters of the bayou.

The big powerboat coasted to a stop. The engine idled beneath her feet. She felt a crawling sensation between her shoulder blades. The immediacies of survival—as in, fending off certain death—had forced her to expose herself to the boat's pilot, in his cockpit aft. She expected to hear the shattering crack of a shot, feel a bullet lance her back.

She wheeled around, sword ready, gleaming like a ray of light in the brilliant sun. The pilot sat with his hands up and his eyes, staring at her in almost mindless horror. She might have been some kind of movie monster emerged from the swamp to kill his mates.

It was, she reflected, no less likely than what he had just seen happen.

Sword in hand she stalked toward him. He got up and turned as if to flee straight astern. There was nothing back there but the aft rail and black water. She darted forward, grabbed him by the back of his green polyester shirt, spun him to face her.

He gibbered. She didn't need him intelligible anyway.

"Listen," she said, grabbing him by the shirt-front so that his terrified face was looking down at hers. "You're dealing with things you can't handle here. You realize that, don't you?"

He just stared at her. He was a young man, maybe early twenties, and seemed fit. But his muscles were as slack as his lips in his fear.

She shook him until his head nodded.

"Fine," she said. "Make sure you tell your bosses that. Do you understand?"

This time he nodded in pathetic haste.

"Great. And tell Sulin the next time I see him he's a dead man. Got that?"

He nodded again. "What are you going to do with me?" he asked.

She frowned. "This," she said, and threw him over the stern.

He landed with a great splash. In a moment his head bobbed up. He flailed furiously with his arms.

"I can't swim!" he screamed at her.

"Learn," she said. She sat down behind the wheel to take the boat back to pick up Jadzia and the scrolls.

21

"And so, using the lightnings stolen from the gods, and the lights that seared at a distance and other wonders, which they had taken from their foes, the brave Athenians defeated the Atlanteans and drove them from their land."

Jadzia sat in a swivel chair staring up at the huge plasma screen in the third-floor lab. The recovered text, the black of carbonization stripped away by software filters, still looked to Annja as much like happenstance scrawls and scratches as writing. Yet Jadzia was clearly in her element.

"Afterwards, when the favor of the gods was withdrawn, the weapons soon ceased to function. Some said the gods disfavored Athens for using the great magics the Atlanteans had wrongly employed, which by rights ought be reserved for the Olympians alone, and that was why the great disaster wrought by the gods struck Greece even as it sank the isle of Atlantis."

She turned to Annja. In the half light her eyes were blue lamps of excitement. "Annja, don't you see? This proves it!"

The Cantonese techs spoke excitedly among themselves in their own language.

"Proves what?" Annja said.

"Why—all of it," Jadzia said. Her cheeks were flushed, her voice breathless. "Atlantis. Unknown energy sources." Her eyes got even wider. "Free energy."

Annja frowned, gazing at the screen as if to suck comprehension out of it by sheer force of will. "I'm not sure I'd go that far," she said uncertainly.

"How far will you go? What more do you need? Don't be so stupid."

Annja's frown cut deeper. After all that had happened, Jadzia was still Jadzia.

WHEN THEY'D FINALLY RETURNED to Joey's Jeep, Annja discovered he had left the driver's door unlocked. In fact the lock was broken. That he hadn't got it fixed and hadn't warned them, but let them solemnly lock all the other doors as if it mattered, seemed to speak volumes about him.

Vearle did not emerge from his shack at the sound of the airboat's return. Annja hoped it didn't mean that Euro Petro goons had paid him a call. She suspected they had not. Sulin had put everything into the trap at Hogue's lodge.

Deep into dusk, when the light was soft and gray and dangerous—because it took the edges and points off things and distorted perspective—Annja found a backwater motel. The clerk was a middle-aged woman who was far more interested in her television than the two self-professed college students from Biloxi, although she did show a grateful smile at being paid cash for a night's accommodations. She didn't bother asking for a license plate number.

Annja got a room around the back, "where it was quiet," as though a car happened down this dismal back road any more than once every ten or twenty minutes. What it really meant was that any EP searchers driving by wouldn't instantly spot their late informant's rather distinctive vehicle. She parked the Grand Cherokee under a big black oak tree to make it hard to spot from an airplane. Or a satellite—she was darned if she wanted their getaway car to turn up in a few hours on Google Earth.

She made the still-weeping Jadzia carry her own bag inside, on general principles. Jadzia was too distraught even to complain. Annja carried the scrolls and the rest of the gear. A pair of full-auto .223s and six full 30-round magazines would go a way toward alleviating those pesky nocturnal fears.

She had suspected Jadzia of being overly theatrical. But when she closed the door with a bump of her butt and let the last bags thump to the thin vomit-colored carpet, the wave of sadness and loss and fear rolled over her like a tsunami. She found herself sitting on the bed with Jadzia. They held each other and cried into each other's shoulders.

Sometime well after dark they cried themselves out. Then Annja took herself mentally by the scruff and shook herself. No matter how she thought things through she could find reasons, and good ones, to blame herself for Tex's death. But he had made his own choices at every stage. No one had held a gun against his head to get him to join her quixotic quest. He had walked with open eyes into a trap laid by someone he had mistakenly trusted.

In the end it didn't matter. What did matter was Tex was dead and Annja and Jadzia were going to have to work fast and smart and most importantly get extremely lucky not to join him in short order.

"So we need to figure out how we're going to survive past tonight," Annja said, as the two women sat on the bed with the TV on and the sound off, eating delivery pizza.

"And avenge Tex," Jadzia said fiercely.

Annja nodded. That seemed right to her, even flying in the face of contemporary morality as it did.

She took a deep breath. "I still think our best chance is to do what we've been trying to do all along—recover as much of the contents of these scrolls as we can and publicize them. The question is how? And also where?"

"Jet propulsion labs in Pasadena is where we sent them," Jadzia said thoughtfully, folding a slice of pizza lengthwise. "They have a CT scanner and an MSI machine."

"So it's a logical choice."

"Too logical," Jadzia said.

"Meaning what?" Annja asked.

"I bet that's where Gus Marshall is," Jadzia said. "Waiting for us in case we decided to head straight there instead of to meet Mr. Hogue."

Annja sighed. "You're right. He's probably hired half the private investigators in the greater L.A. area to keep an eye out for us."

"The police too, maybe."

Annja thrust her chin forward and tilted her head to one side. "Maybe. EP seems to be as reluctant to involve the law as we are. But I agree, we can't take the risk."

"The new university in Shenzhen has CT scanners and multispectral imagers," Jadzia said.

"China?"

"Just inland from Hong Kong, I think. It's sort of a boomtown. There wasn't much there but farming villages twenty years ago. Now it's a big city with a lot of high-tech manufacturing." Jadzia nodded. "They wanted us to send some of our scrolls to them for processing. But there was some kind of trouble, tension with the U.S." Annja knew the United States was a major subsidizer of the governments of both Poland and Egypt, which in turn jointly sponsored the Alexandrian library project. "Some kind of stupid politics."

"I'm with you there," Annja said. She was starting to feel as if they just might have a shot. Not a good one, perhaps—but better than the blank nothing of a future she had seen like a wall ahead a moment before. She thought out loud. "So with China and the U.S. mad at each other—and with China a rival with the big Western companies for oil, with their big boom going on—the Chinese'd be pretty unlikely to be in bed with Euro Petro, wouldn't they?"

Jadzia nodded solemnly. "Sometimes you are not so stupid after all." She upended her soda bottle and took a hefty swig.

"Uh, thanks."

Jadzia was frowning when she lowered the big plastic bottle. "But we have a problem," she said, wiping her mouth with the back of her hand. "It takes forever to get visas for the People's Republic."

Annja's face lit up in a great big smile. "Not necessarily," she said. "The network has a good working relationship with the national government, as well as Guangdong Province's. The Communist party bosses, too. And by that I mean, massive bribery."

"The universal language," Jadzia said.

"IT DOES SEEM TO CLEAR UP one thing that was bothering me," Annja said, studying the ancient text on the screen of the third-floor laboratory in Shenzhen.

"What's that?" Jadzia asked.

"How the Athenians could possibly have defeated Atlantis, if the Atlanteans really had all that marvelous high-tech stuff. No matter how brave or resourceful you are, energy-beam weapons are going to confer a pretty decisive advantage over your bronze swords and bull-hide shields. But if the Greeks managed to get hold of some of those weapons—"

"It's what guerrillas always do," Jadzia said. "I need to pee now." And with that bit of oversharing she turned and walked out of the lab.

22

"Annja, we have to go."

She looked up in surprise as Jadzia entered the room in a burble of noise from the corridor outside. There must have been a class change. There seemed to be a huge amount of traffic, moving both ways with unhurried speed. Nobody raised his or her voice but everybody seemed to be talking at once, very intensely. The PA emitted what sounded more like music than intelligible speech to Annja's uneducated ears. The soundproofing in the lab was so good she'd been unaware of the racket.

"What do you mean?" she asked.

But Jadzia only shook her head so hard her

pigtails whipped her round cheeks. "No time." She walked over and grabbed the satchel of scrolls and ran the strap over her shoulder.

The local technicians paid no attention to either foreign woman. Yet another page of text extracted from a burned scroll had just appeared on the big screen. They were high-fiving and chirping and carrying on as if they'd just scored a touchdown.

Jadzia never even glanced at the monitor. She just turned and walked toward Annja.

"But there's a scroll missing," Annja said, belaboring the obvious. She meant the one being run through the multispectral imager.

"Leave it," Jadzia said. "We have to go."

Annja followed her into the hall. "What's going on?" Annja realized the students were moving along the hallway with a more set purpose than seemed normal.

"You and Tex," Jadzia said incongruously. "You made me realize I could die." Her voice sounded more clotted than tense.

"Huh?" Annja was getting annoyed by Jadzia's behavior.

"Hear that announcement?" Jadzia said. They

were halfway to the stairs nearest the computer lab. "They're saying a terrorist threat has been made against this building. Students are to report to designated evacuation points while antiterror forces secure the place."

Annja felt as if a cold hand had clamped down on her. "Euro Petro?"

Jadzia's face crinkled with fury and disgust. "Who else? Bribery really is the universal language, I guess."

Though she was still loath to admit to herself the possibility there might be something to the Atlantis myths, Annja had to accept that someone at Euro Petro was a true believer.

"You're right," she said tautly. "We have to go."

"Where?" Jadzia asked. Her eyes were openly fearful now.

"Somewhere they don't expect."

The classrooms on the right faced the back of the building. Annja grabbed the latch of the nearest door.

She opened the classroom door, stepped quickly inside.

Jadzia followed tentatively. "We're on the second floor," she pointed out.

"Yep," Annja said.

The room was dimly lit with morning light through half-drawn shades. Moving swiftly between the desks, she reached the line of windows on the far side and examined them. They were built to angle open a handspan to permit airflow but no farther. One or two were open, allowing the smells of humid subtropical greenery to eddy in.

"This low down they shouldn't be shatterproof or anything," she said, thinking aloud. She went to the head of the small classroom. The professor's desk was large and heavy. A swivel chair rested just behind it.

Annja hoisted the chair over her head and threw it through the nearest window. The whole casement failed and fell away with a crash.

She stuck her head out into the humid air and looked quickly around. Below her lay a parking lot with a scatter of boxy cars of unfamiliar makes parked near the building. The far side was bordered by a taller-than-head-high hedge.

It marked the northern edge of the campus. Beyond rose the blocky buildings of an industrial park. The sound of traffic was like the rush of a nearby river. On the west end of the lot stood a copse of lychee trees. To the east, Annja's right, a sheltered walkway with soaring, curving concrete pillars holding up an eccentrically angled roof led to a lot exit. She saw no one.

"What now?" Jadzia asked.

"Simple," Annja said, and jumped.

She struck a perfect three-point landing. She hit a bit harder than she'd expected but her powerful legs easily absorbed the impact of the fall.

"Annja!" she heard Jadzia scream.

A strand of hair fell before her eyes as she raised her head. Through the chestnut screen, turned auburn at the edges by the morning sun, she saw a squad of six soldiers in bulky camouflaged battledress trot into view, three to the left side of the parking lot, three to the right, machine pistols angled before them.

She looked up just in time to see the heavy bag

of scrolls plummet down on her. She just managed to raise her hands to field the well-scuffed green-and-purple bag. It slammed into her chest and forced her back a couple of steps.

"You might want to warn me next time," she called up to Jadzia's pale pigtail-framed face.

"What about me?" the girl called back, ignoring the remark.

Annja dropped the satchel to the sidewalk. "Same way as the bag," she said. "I'll catch you."

One thing Annja had to give Jadzia. She didn't allow common sense to hold her back from much. The next thing Annja knew 110 pounds or so of lanky young woman was falling with all the skill and grace of a sock monkey.

She caught the girl and they fell in a heap.

"Are you all right?" Jadzia asked.

"Probably not," Annja said fuzzily. One of Jadzia's extremities had clocked her in the right eye. She stirred her limbs to prove to herself she could. She felt very feeble. "But that won't stop me."

She wondered in passing if Jadzia was showing actual concern for another person—or simple dread at the prospect of being stranded all alone in a parking lot in the People's Republic of China with fifty pounds of hot artifacts and a antiterror unit plus a probable multinational army of corporate thugs about to land on her like an imploded tower.

She realized she couldn't breathe. "Will you… please…get off?"

"Oh." Jadzia scrambled to her feet.

Annja arched her back and jumped up to her feet in an acrobatic recovery. Immediately she swayed and would've fallen flat down had Jadzia, either deliberately helpful or accidentally in the way, not propped her up.

"Okay, that wasn't bright," Annja muttered. "Let's go."

It was sheer bravado. But it worked. She engaged her will. And that, she knew, was a pretty powerful thing.

She took the scrolls from Jadzia. They'd move quicker that way. She led across the lot at a trot for the exits. The soldiers opened fire but were still too far away to do any harm.

Surprisingly the street beyond the hedge was

not full of traffic. What there was ran to a lot more cars and a lot fewer bicycles than Annja had expected.

"What now?" Jadzia asked.

A white-and-red taxi approached from the left. Annja walked right out in its path, faced it squarely and held her right hand out in a stop gesture.

The driver locked up the brakes. The tires squealed. It shuddered to a halt with the chrome of the bumper all but brushing Annja's shins. The stink of burned rubber rose up about Annja, momentarily drowning out the exhaust fumes. Reaction-dizzy, Annja toppled forward. She caught herself with a hand with a thump on the hood. The metal was hot as a stovetop.

"Okay," she said. "Not a good idea."

The driver stuck his head out the window. He had a kind of pushed-in face with somewhat extruded lips that made him look like a cartoon duck, prominent ears that didn't and immense industrial-framed glasses that inspired little confidence in his visual acuity. "What matter you, crazy Western-devil girl? You wan' die?"

"We need a ride," she said.

"You pay American dollar?" he asked without hesitation.

"If you want," she said.

His manner changed immediately. "You crazy girls, need crazy ride. You come to right man. Hop in!"

They did. Annja shoved Jadzia in first, then the scrolls. As she leaned down to follow, Jadzia vented a squeal that went through Annja's head like a red-hot railroad spike.

"Annja! Behind us!"

From a pillared exit two blocks behind the cab, a glossy blue Mercedes sedan was howling through a turn. Despite the violence of the maneuver, not to mention a score of cars in between, a man hung halfway out the front passenger window. The muzzle-flash of his assault rifle was a brilliant dancing spark.

23

Annja dived in headfirst on top of the bag of scrolls. "Drive," she said.

The driver didn't move. Instead he turned around. "You no pay combat pay," he declared firmly.

Annja's hand slid into her pants pocket. She writhed on top of the gym bag and a startled Jadzia, cursing the vanity that made her wear her tight jeans instead of the baggier cargo pants she often wore. After a contortion or two she squeezed out her wallet. Lying fully across Jadzia's lap she fished in it, grabbing some bills.

She came out with at least two hundred dollars and thrust it at the cabbie.

"The same if you get us safe to the Hong Kong airport!" she shouted.

His hand snatched the bills like a mongoose taking a striking cobra. "I your man!" he declared, turning and shifting into Drive. "You call me Rambo now!"

Annja sat up and looked out the back window. The bad news was a second big sedan full of hitmen had blasted out of the gates. The good news was both pursuers were at least momentarily locked up in traffic. Even Shenzhen drivers tended to lose their composure when random full-automatic gunfire sprayed over their heads.

The cab took off as if it had a jet assist. Annja, Jadzia and satchel got jumbled into a heap of synthetic fabric and long, lean feminine limbs. After a few confused, squirming moments they got themselves sorted out, though Annja's left eye socket now throbbed from having gotten Jadzia's elbow in it. At least they'll match, she thought.

Annja looked back again. Their pursuers had sorted themselves out and accelerated, weaving in and out of traffic. Annja had the satchel dumped on her again as their cabdriver did the same thing. She heard the blare of a horn and a big flat-nosed panel truck rushed by the other way, so close the cab actually rocked to its passage.

Traffic actually picked up as they exited the industrial area by the university. But the pursuing vehicles were gaining by dint of truly demented recklessness. For the moment they had quit shooting, anyway.

"What about the army?" Jadzia asked as the cab's darting for position tossed them from side to side. They had finally managed to get their seat belts fastened, which prevented them from crashing into each other at each wild swerve. "Why aren't they chasing us?"

"They may not even know we got away," Annja said. "And having announced the security sweep through the building, I suspect they have to carry through with it."

A sudden crack made them both cringe. They looked back to see a hole in the rear windshield with a white spider of fractured glass around it.

The bullet had apparently passed out the open front passenger window. Somehow it had missed all three occupants.

"Son of a bitch must pay!" the driver screamed in English. He leaned out his own window to throw a finger back at their pursuers, one of whom had pulled momentarily into the opposing traffic lane for a clear shot at them. He turned forward just in time to keep the cab from veering into the front bumper of a cement truck, which passed with the now almost obligatory blare of a horn.

They crossed a bridge over the river that formed the eastern border of the university. The slow water was bright green, with a sort of iridescent sheen to it, like radiator fluid. "It looks just like what Hollywood thinks toxic waste looks like," Annja said.

"Cool," Jadzia said. "Maybe there are mutants."

"Pollution just temporary problem of growth!" cried their cabbie over his shoulder. He glanced in his side mirror as they came off the bridge. "Uh-oh. Bad guys gaining."

They were. The second Mercedes was just a few cars back in the pack.

"Do something," Jadzia hissed urgently.

The cabbie fumbled around in the front seat and shocked Annja when he hauled out a submachine gun. Its cylindrical see-through magazine showed it was mostly full of cartridges.

The cabbie handed it back. "Chang Feng. Very nice."

Maybe Rambo wasn't such a bad name for him, Annja thought.

"What are you waiting for?" Jadzia shouted. The black Mercedes swerved around another little boxy sedan to move in closer. Behind them the blue pursuer also gained ground. "Shoot them."

"I can't," Annja said. "Not until I get a better shot. I'm not going to spray traffic with bullets at random."

"They do!"

"Do you want to be like them?"

"I want to be alive!"

A street angled off at forty-five degrees to their left. The cabbie suddenly cranked the car across two lanes of onrushing traffic and shot up it.

"This isn't the right way," Jadzia complained.

"The border with Hong Kong is east and south of here! We're going northeast."

"Well, we just lost the black Mercedes," Annja said, looking back. "We need to lose both before anything else happens. Anyway, the airport's on an island pretty much south of the university. We've been heading away all this time."

They had come into a zone of flats between steep hills. Beyond them rose factories, sculptures of tanks and pipework and chimneys, all lustily belching black smoke and white steam.

"Black car back behind us," Jadzia said. Her voice rose an octave. "Here comes the blue one! Shoot! Shoot!"

Annja twisted in her seat. The traffic had thinned to next to nothing. The black car was making a move, overtaking rapidly on the left.

"No worries!" the driver chortled. The taxicab accelerated away from the Mercedes.

After a moment the bigger sedan accelerated. Annja thought she could actually hear its engine roar.

"We can't outrun them!" Jadzia wailed.

She and Annja rocked violently forward as the

driver tapped the brakes. Annja's mouth bounced off the passenger's headrest.

"What are you doing?" Jadzia screamed at the driver as the cab jolted and slowed to another hit on the brakes.

The Mercedes shot past them. A man hung half out the window again. He grabbed the frame, trying to twist to shoot back without falling out of the vehicle.

The cab accelerated again. The gunner was actually facing away from it, with his rump all but sticking out the window. They scooted past.

This time she definitely heard the Mercedes' engine growl furiously as it sped up to run them down. "Now driver watch only us," the cabbie sang out. "Too bad for them."

Annja glanced toward him, then did a second take. A train bridge crossed the road ahead of them, complete with a bloodred and sunflower-yellow-painted locomotive creeping across it, pulling open-topped cars piled perilously high with what looked to Annja like rusting chunks of scrap metal.

As they approached the bridge the Mercedes

surged up alongside. Annja saw the gunman grinning over the sights of his bullpup assault rifle at her. She started to raise the Chang Feng, knowing she was too late.

The cabbie threw the wheel hard left. The cab sideswiped the Mercedes. The enemy driver probably flinched reflexively away from a car slamming into his. The black Mercedes rammed head-on into the concrete bridge support.

It telescoped with a terrible grinding screech, and a cloud of white steam rose from its ruptured radiator. Through the white puff Annja saw the gunner's body snapped suddenly sideways.

She gulped down sour bile. A human body wasn't meant to bend that way.

The cabbie uttered a triumphant rebel yell. Jadzia echoed him piercingly, pumping her fist.

"Not so fast," Annja said. "Here comes the other one."

They were driving between factory buildings, with almost no other cars on the road. The blue Mercedes was overtaking them quickly. This time Sulin himself leaned out the passenger window, white hair whipping in the wind, aiming an assault rifle one-handed.

"Your turn to do something," the cabbie shouted. "Better make snappy!"

"Roll down your window," Annja told Jadzia.

"What?"

"Do it!"

Jadzia cranked the window down, using both hands. Annja flung herself across the girl's lap and stuck her right arm and head out.

The blue Mercedes was swinging out to come alongside. Sulin wanted to make sure of his shot, it seemed.

The cab masked him from Annja. She lined up the red-dot sight on the shadowy figure of the driver and pumped out a 2-round burst, followed by another.

The windshield cracked as four holes appeared in front of the driver. The Mercedes continued to overtake them. Then it suddenly veered away left.

A meaty thump came from the rear of the cab. Annja felt the vehicle rock. The pursuing Mercedes went off the road into the ditch. It rolled over once, continuing to slide forward at a great rate of speed.

"He's on the car!" Jadzia screamed.

"What?"

"Sulin! He's on the roof!"

The cabbie hit the brakes hard. The white-haired assassin failed to fly off the front. The cabbie shifted his narrow butt into the passenger seat, improbably, and continued to steer from there as the taxi slowed.

Bullet holes appeared in the middle of the roof. Bullets struck the inside of the driver's door. If the cabbie hadn't moved he would have been shot in the head and shoulders.

"I saw that in a movie!" the cabbie crowed.

"Annja! Do something!" Jadzia cried.

She aimed the Chang Feng at the roof, pulled the trigger. Nothing happened. With no idea how to clear a jam in the unfamiliar weapon, Annja let it drop.

Still lying across Jadzia's lap, Annja held her hand tipped forward at an angle between the front seats. "Stay put," she advised the cabbie. She focused.

The sword sprang into being, angled upward. To Annja's relief it cleared the arm the driver used to steer the slowing vehicle.

Another burst ripped down into the driver's seat. Bits of stuffing flew up to drift like gnats around the inside of the car. Annja dropped her hands so she could bring the tip of the sword to the holes in the roof. Then she thrust up with both hands on the hilt.

With a crunching sound the sword pierced the roof of the cab. The cabbie ducked under her arm back into his seat to take better control of the cab.

For a moment Annja wondered if her blow had gone true. Would another burst rip through the ceiling, kill the driver and leave them helpless? Or kill her—or Jadzia, whose safety was in her hands?

A red drop ran down the side of the blade. Then another. Then a scarlet stream poured down to wet her hands.

IT STRUCK ANNJA AS strange that a factory that must have been recently built could already be derelict. But as he pulled in out of sight from the road behind a huge blocky concrete structure, the cab bouncing across a parking lot already cracked and heaved by weeds sprouting through it, Rambo the cabbie explained that businesses died off as quickly as they sprang into being in boomtown Shenzhen.

The cab stopped. Annja let go of the sword. It vanished, allowing a brief rain of blood just beginning to congeal to fall to the floor of the cab. Some of it fell on Annja's hand and forearm. She grimaced.

But if you're willing to shed it, you'd better be willing to wear it, she told herself grimly.

They got out. Sulin was still breathing, shallowly and irregularly. Jadzia helped Annja ease him off the roof and gently to the ground. Blood was crusting around his nostrils and streamed down his chin.

"You think you've won," he wheezed. "You cannot win. You have made it personal."

"Don't talk," Annja said, kneeling beside him. "We'll call an ambulance for you."

"What's this? Mercy to a fallen foe?" The beautiful, too-fine features twisted in a sneer.

"Fool yourselves if you will. Don't try to fool me. I'm dying. I have seen enough death to know."

"All right," Annja said. She stood. "What did you mean, it's personal, then?"

"The director," he said with a ghastly bubble running through his asthmatic wheezing. "He has commanded that you two be hunted down and killed at any cost. However long it takes."

"What about the scrolls?" Jadzia asked. She was calm. It bothered Annja slightly. Was there something wrong with her? Or was she merely on emotional overload?

Why don't I feel more? she wondered. And then she realized she did feel something—empty. Utterly drained. Of fear, as well as hope.

Sulin shook his head weakly.

"Regardless of what befalls the scrolls," he said, "no one is permitted to defy the company as you have." He smiled as if in contemptuous amusement, whether at them or his own employer, Annja couldn't tell. Probably both, she guessed.

"Run if you will," he said. His voice was a

whisper. "You cannot get away. You will only die tired. But I can help you escape them."

"Tell me," Annja said.

He raised his right hand with obvious effort. "Come close," he said in a voice like the ghost of the last wind of autumn.

She frowned but knelt again and leaned down. His breath was thready on her cheek.

"I have your escape," he said, "in my hand."

With blinding speed his left hand shot toward her neck. She caught him by the wrist. The needle point of a stiletto hovered half an inch from her carotid artery.

"Damn you!" he growled. The violet eyes were wide and staring. "Who are you?"

"Your worst enemy," she said.

He arched his back. She felt him die. All the tension and strength flowed out of him with the life force.

Gently she laid his hand, still clutching the stiletto, across the front of his immaculately tailored dove-gray suit coat. She gazed at the red morass from the wound the sword had made in his chest.

She stood. For a moment she looked down at the sculpted elfin features. Despite his final spasm he looked perfectly at ease, perhaps for the first time in his life.

"What demons drove you?" she asked under her breath. "What kind of thoughts ran through your head?"

She looked up to see Jadzia's cheek glistening with tears.

"I hate him," the girl said. "Why did it hurt to watch him die?"

"Be glad," Annja said. "It means we're both still human."

She looked to their driver, who stood with arms akimbo regarding his poor battered car. She expected him to demand a prodigious payment to make good the damage to his cab. But his eyes were bright and his cheeks flushed from the chase and running battle.

"It all right," he said. "Insured!"

Annja raised an eyebrow. "Against crash damage, spilled blood and bullet holes? That seems like a lot to ask of an insurance company. Even for a wide-open town like Shenzhen."

He laughed. "Oh, no," he said. "For theft! Car disappear, so sad. Shenzhen full of thieves!"

"What about him?" Jadzia asked, indicating Sulin. "We can't leave him here."

For practical more than sentimental reasons Annja agreed.

"No problem," the cabbie said. "You pay?"

Annja sighed. "I pay." He did save our lives, she reminded herself.

He opened the trunk and produced, to Annja's astonishment, a box of garbage bags. "We stuff him in trunk. I know all about it. I'm a big *Sopranos* fan. I leave car somewhere hidden before I report stolen. Dump him—just like New Jersey!"

24

"We have to change our strategy," Annja told Jadzia.

They sat in the departure area of Hong Kong's relatively new Chek Lap Kok Airport on Lantau Island, waiting to board the afternoon flight that would carry them to Kuala Lumpur. It was the first available flight out of Hong Kong and China. Annja had avoided rousing suspicion by paying with a credit card in a phony name that Roux had provided to her on a previous mission.

"What do you mean?" Jadzia asked, half defiant.

"We're out of resources," Annja said, "out of

places to turn. There are only a few places with the ability to transcribe the scrolls, and they're all barred to us. We have no way of getting the secrets of the scrolls to the world at large."

Jadzia's shoulders slumped. "What can we do, then? Isn't that our only chance?"

Annja's own shoulders rose as she took a deep breath. "There may be a way to save ourselves," she said. "Maybe. And if it works it will definitely keep the scrolls out of the hands of our enemies." She shook her head. "But that's all. Beyond that we're stymied. Unless you can think of something we haven't tried."

Jadzia looked at her bleakly. Her mouth worked as if trying to shape words she didn't want to say. Her eyes brimmed and overflowed with tears.

Annja put her arms around her as Jadzia sobbed into her shoulder, soaking her blouse.

She was suddenly struck by the heaviest, most devastatingly complete sense of loneliness she had ever known.

She was isolated. She had a unique role, which she had no more chosen than her parents had chosen to go away from her. It set her apart from the rest of humanity—with a few exceptions, perhaps no more than two, and they were as alien to her as to everybody else on the planet. She saw with sudden clarity how her new role might preclude her from forming any kind of lasting relationships.

It came to her lips to tell Jadzia that, to seek the solace of at least sharing her burden.

But she knew she could not share and remain true to herself. She was a uniquely powerful being. Roux had certainly intimated as much, and while she knew full well he would twist the truth or outright lie as suited his own agenda, she also sensed he was right.

And that power, as the cliché ran, imposed upon her a crushing weight of responsibility. She *couldn't* tell Jadzia of her own loneliness and isolation. Not just because the girl was a mere child, although she was, emotionally. Annja simply wouldn't slough off her burdens on anyone else.

And so Annja sat there as the airport throngs surged heedlessly past, doing her best to soothe this child who needed her.

At last Jadzia's sobbing ebbed. She eased away from Annja, smoothed tears from her face and said almost matter-of-factly, "What do you have in mind?"

Annja took out a cell phone. She had bought it from a friend of Rambo the adventure-loving cabdriver. It was a pay-as-you-go phone, the contact said—legal, he said. She was in no position either to know or care. The one thing that mattered was the one thing that was sure—when she used it no board would light up anywhere in the vast web of Euro Petro's spider empire pinpointing the whereabouts of Annja, Jadzia and the lost Atlantis scrolls.

She punched a sequence of numbers she remembered better than she cared to.

"MASTER GARIN," a voice said over the intercom.

Garin Braden scowled. "Hoskins," he said sharply, "I gave orders I was not to be disturbed."

"If I may be so bold as to say so, sir," the butler said over the intercom, unperturbed, "you also directed in no uncertain terms that you should be notified at once of the receipt of any communication from one Ms. Annja Creed."

His coal-black eyebrows rose. "So I did. And I take it we are in receipt of such a communication?" He made his tone arch, to show he was mocking his butler's overly elaborate elocution.

"We are indeed, sir. A telephone call."

"Come ahead, then," he said.

A moment later his man's man entered bearing an opened flip phone on a silver platter.

"Thank you, Hoskins," Garin said, accepting it as the servant stooped. Hoskins straightened and walked from the room. Garin settled back in his chair.

"Annja? Are you there?"

"Garin?"

"Unless you hit the wrong speed-dial button when you were calling out for pizza, whom did you expect, my girl?"

"Look, I don't have much time. I'm in trouble."

"Then why waste my time belaboring the obvious? You're always in trouble. Although I grant it must be deeper than normal, for you to call me."

"It is. I—I have a deal for you."

"I'm all about the making of deals. Does this involve your surrendering the sword to me?"

"No."

"Pity. But I find myself in a receptive mood. Bored, to put not too fine an edge to it. What do you have in mind?"

A pause. That surprised him. Annja Creed was not given to hesitancy, in his experience.

"I can offer you extraordinarily valuable resources," she said, "if you will do me a favor."

"You can't tell me precisely what resources?"

"No."

"How valuable?"

"Beyond your wildest dreams of avarice."

"My dreams are quite expansive, my dear. But I respect your judgment, at least in such matters. What favor?"

"Get somebody off our backs."

"Our?"

"Mine. And a friend."

"Consider it done. For considerations offered. Whom can I do for you?"

"Euro Petro."

After a rather lengthy silence he vented a half-voiced whistle. "You don't do things by half measures, do you, Annja? That's the European

Union you're talking about. Even for me that's a heavy hitter."

"Then you can't help me?"

"Don't try to manipulate my ego. That was last done with any success shortly before the close of the eighteenth century, under circumstances I prefer not to discuss. If there's something I know I can't do, rest assured I feel no compulsion to try."

"Cut the crap, Garin. Will you or won't you?" Annja said.

His laughter was long and loud and rich. "You delight me, Annja. Of all the men and women who think they know the extent of my power, only the merest handful would dare talk to me like that. And only you and Roux know the *real* nature of my capabilities. How is our old mentor, by the anyway?"

"The same annoying, self-righteous old fart as always. Please, Garin."

"Very well. Since you said the magic word, it's a deal." He grinned at the phone. "To tell you the truth, you *have* tweaked my ego, girl. There are so few worthy challenges left to me. How could I pass this one by?"

25

"Will your friend really help us?" Jadzia asked.

Annja scowled. "He's not really a friend."

They walked by night among the quaint and mostly authentic colonial buildings of central Kuala Lumpur. They seemed to exist in a hidden valley walled in on all sides by canyons of steel and concrete. In one direction the colossal Petronas dominated the immediate skyline. They looked to Annja's eye like a pair of huge rocket ships linked together. In another rose the Kuala Lumpur Tower, nearly as tall as the Petronas twins. It resembled the world's largest stalk of asparagus. Cars and buses hissed along narrow old-town streets that meandered like streams as if in contrast to the geometric exactitude of the skyscrapers.

Jadzia looked at Annja with a spark of interest. It was good to see, after the listlessness the girl had displayed since they'd left Shenzhen.

"A lover?" Jadzia teased.

Annja adjusted the strap of the satchel of scrolls on her shoulder and let out a reflexive chuff of laughter. "I'd say 'he wishes,' but I'm not even sure that's true."

"What about you? Do you wish? Is he a sexy man? A beautiful man?"

"Yes. I guess he is. He's a very powerful man. He's unique."

"So why don't you sleep with him?"

She just shook her head, tight-lipped. Garin Braden was attractive, no question, with his commanding eyes, superb physique and charisma to make the curtains sway when he entered a room. The truth was Annja found it hard to get really intimate with someone who, at any given moment, might decide to try to kill her. It didn't seem politic to mention that to Jadzia in connec-

tion with someone on whom both women currently relied to save their lives.

Leaving a compulsively neat little square with
palm trees and flowers in planters in the middle
and copper-domed buildings around the fringes,
they entered a more modern section of the city.
And shortly, down a street blocked by concrete
traffic barriers, they came to a wire perimeter
surrounding a half-finished building.

A crash sounded from behind them. They
both turned. A heavy truck had just bulled its
way between two waist-high barriers and was
roaring down the street at them.

"Oh, no," Jadzia said.

Annja grabbed the satchel with one hand and
Jadzia's wrist with the other. "Come on," she
said, and raced inside the wire. The truck grum-
bled to a halt behind them with a sound like the
tail end of an avalanche.

A pair of uniformed guards with billed caps
and showy white Sam Browne belts came running out of a security shack near the entrance to
the half-built building. "Stop! You cannot come
in here."

Rippling cracks sounded to either side of Annja. The two guards folded like collapsing cardboard cutouts.

Annja looked back over her shoulder and almost stumbled. A burly figure swaggered in the gate with a bow-legged roll. Dark-clad men flanked him, holding suppressed submachine guns to their shoulders.

Jadzia looked too. "Marshall!" she exclaimed. She yelped in terror as she stumbled on a piece of rubble.

Annja would not let her fall. Jadzia cried out as Annja pulled ruthlessly on her arm, barely slowing her stride. She got her sneakers under her and followed with ungainly flapping steps, into the darkness of the building's heart.

"I HEAR THEM!" Jadzia said. "They are below us!"

Her panted words echoed between the raw concrete slabs of roof and floor and the metal sheathing on the outside of the building. The two women had run up a dozen stories of temporary steel stairs with only the most perfunctory kind of safety rail. Fortunately, small amber lights clamped at irregular intervals gave enough illumination that neither woman had put a foot wrong enough to plummet back down.

The drumbeats of feet, the shouts of men's voices, even the panting of their breath came echoing up the deep well.

"We better keep going," Annja said.

"But where? There's nowhere to go but up."

"You're right," Annja said. "But it's not as if we've had much choice."

"Then where are we going? Are we just climbing to prolong the inevitable?"

"To look for somewhere to make a stand," Annja said.

"What kind of stand?" Jadzia demanded. "I thought you left the gun back with the cabdriver."

"I did," she said.

"So what happens when you find someplace you like?"

"Ambush," Annja said. "Classic recourse of the weak and hunted."

She glanced over to see Jadzia screwing up

her face to say something cutting. But she simply nodded. "You're right," she said.

They had a way to go before they ran out of building. But they were running out of options. Jadzia was right—ultimately all that lay up this way was roof. Or actually the topmost floor slab, sixty or seventy stories farther up, with a giant crane clamped to it.

The floors they had just passed had been bare, to judge from what Annja could see. While they did offer plenty of deep darkness, she had to assume their pursuers had some kind of night-vision gear. Under the circumstances, flashlights would be all they'd need to ferret out their quarry.

"We need terrain," Annja said.

"Meaning what? We're in a building."

"Stuff to hide behind."

"Oh."

They reached a new landing.

"How about here?" Jadzia said, looking around. By the amber gleam of a utility light Annja saw a promising plenitude of boxy shapes—portable generators, tool chests on wheels, worktables.

Either more internal work was being done on this floor than those immediately below for some reason, or it was a designated shop. "Perfect," she said, starting away from the stairs.

"Wait," Jadzia said. "Give me the scrolls."

"Really, they're easy for me to carry. Although I have to admit my hips've gotten pretty sore from the bag bouncing off them at every step."

"No," Jadzia said. "Give me the bag so you're free to hit people."

With more relief than she cared to admit, she peeled the strap off her shoulder and handed the satchel to the girl. Then, summoning the sword, just in case, she led the way among the meaty chunks of equipment, turned by the darkness to solid black.

Too late she became aware of a shadow-blur of motion from her left. An impact against the back of her skull filled it with a red explosion, and then a white radiance as blinding as the sun.

26

Annja came back to herself blubbering incoherent words as she lay on her back on a stretcher. She looked over quickly to see Jadzia lying beside her. The girl was in the same shape she was. From the sound penetrating her aching head, Annja realized they were in a helicopter.

"Hello, miss," a British fellow was saying.

A woman knelt beside Annja and shone a light in both her eyes. "Pupils both the same size, you'll be pleased to know," she said in English with a singsong Malay accent. "Sit up for me, please, if you can." She was small and brown and spare, with a red crescent in a white circle patch sewn to the breast of her green jumpsuit.

Annja obeyed. As the Malaysian woman began to probe the blood-matted hair at the back of her head with gloved fingers, something struck Annja. "Wait—are you a Malaysian search-and-rescue team?"

"Oh, no," the medic said from outside of Annja's field of view. "The rest of the team are not even Malaysian."

"Annja!" Jadzia began to struggle frantically. A woman tried to restrain her. The blond girl batted at her weakly. "Annja, do something. They're Euro Petro!"

With a cattle-prod jolt of horror Annja saw the distinctive blue logo on the patch on her rescuer's jumpsuit. Looking around wildly she saw the others wore them, too. She also noticed that every one of the five people in view, except the medic, wore a holstered sidearm.

"What's going on?" Annja said.

The Englishman shrugged apologetically. "You are being rescued," he said, "from what I gather were criminals hired by renegade elements of the very corporation that employs us. Shocking, the things that go on."

He sounded sincere. Annja remembered the anthro prof at college who had told her, "Once you can fake that, you've got it made." Best not to go there, she told herself.

"Jadzia, relax," she said.

"How can you trust them?" The girl allowed herself to be pressed gently but insistently back down on the stretcher.

Annja felt a stinging at the back of her head as the Malaysian woman swabbed her wound with alcohol.

"Because we're still alive," she said.

THE HELICOPTER HOVERED then flared to a landing. Carrying water bottles that had been pressed into their hands by their briskly solicitous rescuers—or captors—the two women were helped out of the helicopter.

It took a moment for Annja to get her bearings. They were on a dark ridge, with waving shadowy trees all around. To one side the sky was lit by a glow that Annja realized could only come from Kuala Lumpur itself.

The friendly Englishman set the bag of scrolls down by Annja's feet. "A pleasure, miss," he said. Then he climbed back into the helicopter, which promptly leapt up into the sky, wheeled east, tipped its snout down and flew away over the city.

A figure approached, tall and slim, with suit-coat tails whipping in the wind of the helicopter's departure.

"Good evening, ladies," Mr. Thistledown said. His bony face was all smiles, as usual. "I am glad to see you both in such tip-top shape, considering your recent terrible ordeal."

He said it as if the "terrible ordeal" had nothing to do with him, as if they had just been plucked from the rim of an erupting volcano.

"And you are?" Jadzia asked suspiciously.

"This is Mr. Thistledown. Mr. Thistledown, this is Jadzia Arkadczyk," Annja said.

He bowed. "Such a very great pleasure to meet you, Ms. Arkadczyk. An honor, if I may say so, to meet one so very young, yet so accomplished in such fields as cryptology and ancient languages."

Jadzia gave Annja a somewhat wild look. Annja shrugged.

"And now, if you please," he said. He gestured back along the ridge top with a knobbly hand. Looking that way, Annja saw a large tent faintly lit from within. Several men stood nearby.

Annja shouldered the bag of scrolls. She and Jadzia accompanied Thistledown toward the tent.

"What happened to Marshall?" Annja demanded. She wasn't in a mood to be polite.

"He and Mr. Sulin were a little too enthusiastic in their pursuit. Under the circumstances, he left us small choice but to act most precipitously. He has been dealt with appropriately."

Annja wasn't sure she wanted to know what that meant.

Jadzia opened her mouth to question that. Relentlessly smiling, Thistledown held up his hand. "It is, I fear, not my place to discuss corporate policy—any more than it is to make it. Oh, my, not my place indeed. And now, if you will permit me the honor—"

He gestured toward the broad, tapering back of a tall man who stood silhouetted against the city lights. The horizon glowed in a million points of light, as if the sky above were merely a pale, diffuse reflection of the real stars below.

"I'd like to introduce you to our new director, Mr. Garin Braden."

The man turned to them and approached, grinning, holding out his hand. Annja felt her knees buckle with mingled relief and trepidation.

"Oh, my God," Jadzia whispered. "He's gorgeous."

Somewhat weakly Annja shook the huge, square hand. As always it felt as if it had been sculpted out of seasoned oak.

"New director?" she asked.

He shrugged. "If you can't beat 'em, buy in, as I always say. At least for the last century or two. And if I'm going to buy in, why not at the top? I couldn't have helped you two much as a mail-room clerk, now, could I?"

"What happened to the old director?" Jadzia asked suspiciously.

"Ah," Mr. Thistledown said. "I fear Herr

Direktor Sinnbrenner is no longer with us. The rest of the board determined he had engaged in conduct quite inappropriate to the role of the consortium. He has accordingly been terminated."

Garin put his hand on Annja's shoulder. She tried not to think about the sensation it produced. He guided her away from Thistledown and the others who stood in the shadows. Jadzia followed. Annja suspected she was determined not to miss anything.

She became aware the hilltop was ringed by a discreet but heavily armed security detail. Even if Jadzia and I weren't utterly wrung out we'd have little chance of escape, she thought. Especially with Garin on hand. He was probably more dangerous than the whole guard force.

He looked to her. "And now, I believe you have something for me."

"Why should we give it to you?" Jadzia flared. "You are supposed to be Annja's friend. But you went over to *them*."

"Did you really describe me as your friend, Annja dear?"

"Not exactly." To Jadzia she said, "Don't you

see? We're in his power. He can simply take what he wants by force."

"Ah, but I won't," he said. "You wrong me, Annja. You should know me as a man of my word." Then he smiled. It was not an altogether pleasant expression. "Besides, force is unnecessary. Come."

He escorted them into the tent. A large-screen plasma TV had been set up against the far wall, hooked to the video output from a notebook computer resting on a camp table. Garin nodded to the young woman who sat at the keyboard.

The screen lit up with a succession of brief video clips. "I know him—" Jadzia burst out, as a popular magician appeared. With his trademark boisterous self-assurance he debunked and ridiculed claims a place called Atlantis ever existed, or had any mystic secrets to be discovered.

He gave way to the Legend Smashers, a pair of wisecracking pyrotechnics experts from a basic-cable rival of *Chasing History's Monsters*. They showed, with a complicated-looking experiment, how zero-point energy extraction could never work. They were followed by other clips in the same vein, including a solemn cable-news channel report revealing a scheme by an American archaeologist and a Polish language expert to take advantage of their lucky escape from an Islamic terror attack on their dig in Alexandria to scam gullible investors out of billions for nonexistent secrets of ancient technology.

"But these sequences look real," Jadzia said, awestruck.

"They are real," Garin said. "They're in the can. Just waiting to be shown. Would you care to see more?"

Annja looked at Jadzia. The girl's face was white as a sheet.

"I think that's enough," Annja said. "Isn't that a lot of expense to go to as a contingency?"

Mr. Thistledown had accompanied them into the tent. Now his ever-present smile broadened. "Young lady, it cost my former employers substantially more to subsidize the antinuclear power movement of the seventies and eighties."

"In any event," Garin said, "none of this

should be necessary. I've fulfilled my end of the bargain, after all."

Annja sighed. "I suppose you have, at that."

"Don't look so grim," he said. "Either of you. As it happens, I'm feeling generous. Very, very generous."

"Why's that?" Annja asked with a narrow-eyed look.

"It took all my available liquidity to swing the purchase of enough stock to make me majority private holder of EP. But as a result of doing so I've already doubled my net worth, and stand to increase my wealth exponentially in a remarkably short time. I really feel I owe you ladies a finder's fee."

"The scrolls?" Annja asks.

"They will be properly conserved, I assure you," Thistledown said. "What's more, Ms. Arkadczyk's position in Alexandria awaits her return. Our new director—" he nodded toward Garin, who was visibly gloating "—has graciously arranged for Euro Petro to take over funding of the library recovery project. As many surviving members of your team as are willing will be brought back onboard. With, of course, additional staff hired by us."

"Including site supervisors?" Annja asked.

"Naturally."

"I want something, too," Annja said.

Garin arched a brow. "Aside from getting the monkey, if I may speak unkindly of the dead, off the back of you and your friend?" He sighed theatrically. "Ah, well. Some people are never satisfied. What?"

"A man named Leo built an ultralight airplane by himself. It was named *Ariel*. Tex and I rented it to rescue Jadzia and we lost it. I want it replaced."

Garin chuckled. "I can arrange that quite cheaply. By remarkable coincidence, a hand-built ultralight aircraft sporting a most unfortunate paint job, I'm given to understand, turned up on one of our properties in the North Sea. A former oil rig I am told EP uses to conduct meteorological observations. They recently experienced some kind of terrible accident, but the aircraft in question is unharmed. Would this Leo person accept that aircraft in exchange for his lost pet, do you think?"

Annja smiled weakly. "I suspect so. Oh, one other thing. Tex Winston's body must be returned to his parents—"

"Yes, in Idaho. As of four hours ago, confirmed by e-mail. A heroic end to a colorful career. A pity that his brave sacrifice of his own life was unable to save Amon Hogue and his nephew from being murdered by a particularly brutal home-invasion gang. But he appears to have taken out several of the bandits before he died. Small consolation to his parents, I'm sure. But they do know that he died a hero."

Annja felt a stinging in her eyes. "Thank you, Garin."

"My pleasure. Is there anything else you'd like from me? For me to cut off my right hand, perhaps?" He held out a hand. "And now, ladies—the scrolls, if you please."

Tears of frustrated rage rolled down Jadzia's cheeks. "But what if they really do hold the secret of unlimited energy?" she said. "Aren't you at least curious?"

Thistledown clucked indulgently. "Young lady, we already know what works. Some quite astonishing things, really. Now, please hand over the scrolls."

Annja let the satchel's strap slide off her shoulder. Stooping slightly, she placed it on the ground between her and the girl.

"It needs to be your choice, Jadzia," she said. "Whatever you decide—even if it's to go out in a blaze of glory—I'll back you."

Jadzia turned and clung to her, crying. At last she recovered a measure of control and lifted her face to Annja, who smiled.

Jadzia turned, grabbed up the satchel and thrust the ancient scrolls toward Garin's broad chest.

"Take them, then," she said fiercely. "But if you ever harm my friend Annja, a terrible, terrible fate will befall you."

Garin arched a brow toward Annja.

"Better listen to her," Annja said. "She has the gift."

James Axler
Outlanders®

SKULL THRONE

RADIANT EVIL

Buried deep in the Mayan jungle amidst a civilization of lost survivors and emissaries of the dead, lies a relic that hides secrets to the prize—planet Earth. In sinister hands, it guarantees complete and absolute power. Kane and the rebels have just one chance to stop a rogue overlord from seizing glory, but must face an old enemy to stop him.

Available May 2007, wherever you buy books.

GOLD EAGLE ®

GOUT41

JAMES AXLER

DEATH LANDS®

Sky Raider

Raw determination in a land of horror…and hope

In the tortured but not destroyed lands of apocalyptic madness of Deathlands, few among the most tyrannical barons can rival the ruthlessness of Sandra Tregart. With her restored biplane, she delivers death from the skies to all who defy her supremacy — a virulent ambition that challenges Ryan Cawdor and his band in unfathomable new ways.

Available June 2007 wherever books are sold.

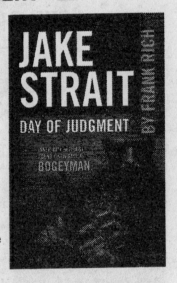

TAKE 'EM FREE

2 action-packed novels plus a mystery bonus

NO RISK

NO OBLIGATION TO BUY